MELAQUE MURDER CLUB

EDMOND GAGNON

Edmond Gagnon Author

MELAQUE MURDER CLUB

CHAPTER ONE

Washed Up

Black! He searched his mind but that was the best description he could come up when trying to remember his past. Black like you find in space between the millions of stars in our galaxy. For lack of a better name, scientists call it black matter...but it did matter. How could his memory be totally blank? Surely there should be something there. Was it amnesia?

Light! So bright he couldn't open his eyes. So intense he thought his eyeballs were about to melt. Relaxing the muscles in his eyelids he peered through tiny slits, trying to get his bearings and figure out where he was. Warm water washed over his body, filling the cracks in his eyelids with salty liquid. It stung.

Seawater! He choked on a mouthful of the salty brine. How did he know if he had no memory? Bringing his hands up to his eyes, he gently wiped water from them. Now they were gritty, making things worse...sand. He was on a beach. Once again, he questioned his lack of memory but knowledge of such things.

Hot! Instinct told him to crawl up the sandy grade, away from the water, before it washed over him again. He shook his head violently, in an attempt to clear his eyes and regain his vision. Fuzzy colors appeared...brown sand and blue sky? Shapes became clearer, but nothing was recognizable. His skin was hot...the location felt tropical. He blinked several times, slowly bringing the world into focus.

Voices. Seeking the source, shapes of people appeared. They were pointing in his direction. Checking his surroundings, he realized they were staring at him. Getting to his feet, he noticed he was naked. Others on the beach were not, probably the reason they were gawking.

Instinct took over again and he scampered up the beach to a thicket, taking cover. People still looked and pointed in his direction but they kept their distance. Masked by the brush, he focused on his surroundings. He was definitely on a beach. He knew saltwater was found in oceans. Knowledge without memory, how could that be?

People were scattered along the beach, some frolicking in the rolling waves and others gathered in the shade under umbrellas or palm trees lining the top of the beach. Beyond that, some were eating and drinking in places he believed to be restaurants. He couldn't remember the last time he had consumed any food or water. The thought made him feel parched and hungry.

Seeing everyone else was clothed, he scoped the immediate area for something to cover himself with. There was an orange and yellow piece of material nearby, mostly buried in the sand. A hard tug revealed a discarded or forgotten beach towel. It was large enough to conceal parts of himself others on the beach kept hidden.

Now what? Where was he and how did he get there? Better yet, who was he and why couldn't he remember anything, including his name or where he was from. Surely, he had a name. His body told him it needed food and water but he wasn't sure how to acquire those things. Would other people offer sustenance if he simply asked. Being a stranger in a place completely foreign to him, his gut said they wouldn't.

The gawkers returned to whatever else they were doing before noticing him. He took the long way around the thicket and made his way along the beach. Maybe if he observed the behavior of others, he would know what to do next. They wore different skin tones, some dark and others lighter than his, which was now sunburnt from lying unconscious in the surf.

A parched throat and hunger pangs steered him toward one of the restaurants, where a man was cleaning his catch of the day. Seagulls squawked and hovered around him, anxiously awaiting any scrap that might come their way. He nearly got clipped by a bird swooping down to catch fish guts tossed its way.

Watching the feeding frenzy, he quickly learned it meant a free meal. He snagged a fish head midair before a gull could nab it. The fisherman gave him an odd look. "You could lose a finger that way. If you're hungry, all you had to do was ask." The local held his hand out, offering the stranger a piece of filleted fish.

Knowing the fisherman should be thanked for his generosity, he opened his mouth to speak but nothing came out. His vocal cords didn't respond. They weren't working. Embarrassed, he offered a polite nod. He gazed at a bottle of water nearby. The fisherman smiled and handed it to him. He appeared puzzled when the hungry man popped the raw fish into his mouth and simply walked away.

CHAPTER TWO

Naked Whales

Satisfied I'd written enough for one day, I read over the completed chapter one more time before calling it quits. The new book was progressing well, my next installment in the Abigail Brown crime series. They said, 'write what you know' when I decided to become a novelist. Policing the mean streets of a Canada/U.S. border city for over thirty years, I had many stories to tell.

Checking the clock on my laptop, I decided to make an appearance at the beach. Katie was already there so I thought I'd socialize with her and our friends for a couple hours before my nap. My wife was more the beach person, I preferred swimming in a pool where I could see my feet and whatever else was in the water with me. And I hate sand; that stuff gets everywhere.

The usual suspects were at our table, shaded by a large umbrella perfect for keeping me out of the blazing sun. There were other tables in rows parallel with the shoreline. Ours was blue and yellow, colors representing those owned by Fenix de Melaque, our Seniors' Resort. I was greeted with the usual bows and jokes about rolling out the red carpet to keep my tender tootsies off the sand.

To be a team player, I set aside my quirks about the beach and visited the table about once a week. Big Willy pulled out a double chair and offered me a seat. I took a celebratory bow in return and used my weight to force the seat into the sand. He and I were heavyweights and had broken our share of flimsy plastic chairs so we double-stacked them for strength to avoid falling and spilling our cerveza.

My wife handed me a low carb, low calorie, flavorless beer from our cooler and patted my shoulder as if to say, 'good doggie...here's your treat for coming'. While I settled in, Wanda waived over the candy man, one of many beach vendors who catered to sun-worshiping gringos all day, trying to earn a few pesos. Looking over his cartful of assorted goodies I wondered how they didn't melt in the hot sun.

We chose Melaque, in Mexico, for exactly that reason. The sun ruled the sky every day in winter, keeping the mercury hovering around 85 degrees Fahrenheit. Rain was unheard of that time of year. I pointed to the candied pecans and asked the dude to bag me fifty pesos worth. My beer had evaporated by the time I got a fistful of nuts into my mouth so I helped myself to another cold one.

Oohs and ahs came from a group two tables over. It was a dead giveaway to what was happening out in the bay. Casting my eyes to the horizon I caught the splash and knew the cause. Within seconds a young humpback broke the surface again, a beautiful full breach. Just as the giant mammal splashed down, a second one mimicked the maneuver gaining even more height. Sibling rivalry or a competition of sorts, perhaps?

For a guy who regularly spewed comments like, 'you've seen one whale, you've seen them all', GP seemed impressed. Short for George Patton, his moniker, he was king of one-liners. He didn't let us down during the National Geographic moment. "Look at that young buck...chasing tail at his age...wonder if he smacked his balls on that landing."

The aquatic show continued for about five minutes while the young whales swam further out to sea. Mom broke the surface occasionally as she flanked and kept watch over her offspring. I lost myself in thought while I watched the world travelers heading for the horizon. They were just like us snowbirds, with summer and winter homes in the north and south.

Sticks came up from behind and asked what was going on. She earned her nickname because of the two ski poles she used to walk and remain steady on her feet. Katie pointed out to sea and told her about the whales and asked her if she was feeling any better, switching chairs to let her sit in the shade. Sticks had been ill and missed the steak barbeque the night before.

"A lot better today, thanks. But I can't say the same for Bruce, did he spend the night here at the resort on someone's couch?" The remark caught everyone's attention, soliciting puzzled expressions.

GP answered. "He tied one on last night but stumbled out of here before the party broke up...we assumed he went home."

Wanda chimed in. "It's only two blocks to your place, could he have passed out somewhere along the way? I don't think he could've gotten far in his condition."

Sticks replied. "Not that I know of...you've got me worried now. He's had a lot on his mind lately...with things like the lack of work back home. Money's tight and I don't think we'll be coming back next winter...maybe only a short trip to the Yucatan, to see our granddaughter."

I spoke up. "It's not like he got picked up by the cops and tossed in the drunk tank...I haven't even seen any tourist police this year."

Separate conversations broke out around the table. Willy gave me a concerned look, lifting one eyebrow like Mr. Spock. Katie suggested we do something but no one came up with any suggestions. Sticks was visibly upset. Wanda put a hand on her arm and told her not to worry.

GP laughed out loud. "Sorry, look over there…" He pointed to a naked man on the beach. "Maybe he didn't get the memo…we don't do nude sunbathing here."

Forgetting about poor Bruce for a moment, we all turned to see.

I said, "Looks like he's right out of it…must have been a good party last night if he's just waking up now. Maybe he knows where Bruce is."

Katie punched my arm and gawked at the nude man. "Can't say the water's cold today…no shrinkage there."

I punched her back. The other women giggled and the guys instinctively checked their own packages. The man seemed aware everyone was gawking and he scurried into some bushes on a vacant lot at the top of the beach.

Big Willy barked, "Nah, he's got nothing on us…right, Edmundo?"

That was my adopted Mexican name—we all had one.

"Right. His only looks bigger because he's skinnier and it's not camouflaged by overhanging six-packs like ours."

Everyone laughed. Katie reached over and patted my lap. "Yours is big enough, baby, after I coax it a bit." She smiled.

Sticks had just taken a swig of beer and spewed it across the table, wetting Wanda and Willy.

GP continued laughing. "I believe that big guy…you know what they say about big feet… what size are yours…11 or 12?"

At some point during the penis conversation, we lost track of the naked guy.

CHAPTER THREE

Snatched

Dale was an early riser, even before he retired from his teaching job and moved south to the beach town of Melaque, in Mexico. Some say you wake earlier in your golden years, but Dale was a consistent five to nine guy his whole life, up at the crack of dawn and tucked into bed around the same time the street lights came on.

Donald, his partner of twenty years, was the polar opposite when it came to sack time. In their case they found opposites attract. Having met at a teacher's conference in Toronto, they retired within a year of each other, sold their modest homes and banked over two million dollars. With the low cost of living in Mexico, they lived comfortably in their sunny seaside condo.

Rosco was a short and plump mutt, a rescue dog they picked up when the couple settled into their new digs. Dale had to rush his morning pee before the bitsa (bits of this and bits of that) started barking to go outside. The dog's bladder was in sync with its master's. It wasn't a problem for Dale, who enjoyed the early morning walks. Waking up with the sun, as he liked to say.

He could have walked blindfolded since Rosco had the route all staked out. His first pee stop was next door on the neighbor's rose bush. She was never up early enough to catch the mutt in the act, and constantly complained to the two men how the local climate was too hot for her ever-wilting rose bushes.

Their route took them along the old malecon in Villa Obregon, a run-down section of walkway that skirted the western edge of the lagoon. Dale enjoyed the serenity and marveled at how the snowy egrets glowed in the morning light. They glided gracefully over the water like angels sent down from heaven. Purple flowers topped large swaths of water hyacinths, adding to the Garden of Eden effect.

Like the antagonist in the biblical story, Laguna del Tule had its own serpents. Crocodiles lurked in the shallows and reeds. Dale had seen many of them in the past and he kept Rosco on a leash for exactly that reason. There was even an old warning sign at one entrance to the path, with a picture of a little dog in a croc's mouth.

Since Rosco wasn't a fan of the water, he liked to walk on the dry side of the path where he could freely sniff the remnants of other canine droppings and try to outdo them by leaving his own mark. Dale constantly wondered how such a small dog could store so much urine. Rosco was a piss machine.

A flutter of wings caught the man's attention. A great blue heron took flight from the water's edge, lumbering into the air like a giant cargo plane. When Dale looked back down there was nothing but an empty leash in his hand. Rosco was gone. Dale's heart leapt into his throat, as if trying to escape his chest. There were ripples in the water where the heron had taken off.

Frantic, he leaned over for a closer look, and called out to Rosco. Dale was about to jump in when he saw something moving below the water's surface. He called out again and reached for his second-best friend. It was the last thing he said or did.

CHAPTER FOUR

Dead Soldiers

Back at our suite, Katie jumped in the shower and I hit the sack for my afternoon nap. We chatted a bit more about Bruce and his strange disappearance, before I watched her bare bottom wiggle its way to the bathroom. I hadn't hit the wall yet so I decided to read a chapter of John Grisham's, A Painted House. Over a hundred pages in, I was still waiting for something to happen.

The smell of bacon woke me up. Katie was prepping her Caesar salad when I walked into the kitchen. "You can light the barbeque when you wake up...pork chops are ready to go when you are." I grabbed a still-hot piece of bacon from the pan. "Get out of there...I hope you burn your tongue. GP and Helen have those pork necks he likes and she's making dessert."

"There kind of bony but I like them too...what's for dessert?"

"I don't know...she didn't say. Does it matter?"

"Nope." Checking my email on the laptop to see if anyone missed me, Facebook offered nothing new except for lots of compliments and comments on my latest post 'Five Door Friday'. I posted a variety of images captured on my morning walks, gathering a group of door fans along the way.

I wandered out to the barbeque and saw GP had it fired up and smoking heavily enough to attract the local fire department.

"Cranked it up to burn shit off the grill. This propane baby goes up to about six hundred degrees."

"Wish my natural gas one at home did that...the searing station barely does the trick." I walked over to the mini fridge behind the bar. "Shit, I don't have any beer left."

"Take one of mine."

"Thanks, I already did."

We sat and stared at the wafting smoke for a minute before I broke the silence. "I wonder if Bruce found his way home yet."

"He was a train wreck when he left here." GP nodded toward the two empty tequila bottles, new additions to a row of dead soldiers. "Could have been any one of us after our little barbeque last night. I'm still a bit fuzzy. This should help..." He took a sip of scotch, something he normally didn't get into until after dinner.

"Those steaks were awesome...yours musta been two inches thick. Katie says you wanted to throw Bruce's on the ground and wear it as a sandal."

GP laughed. "What a piece of crap...nothing but grizzle. Mine was AAA from Alberta...not that national shit they call beef here. I don't know what they do to their meat...it doesn't taste real."

My mind wandered. I scanned the back of the beer bottle I was drinking. "Hey, are they recycling glass here now? Thought I saw empties in the big bin on the boulevard."

"Only the clear stuff...I think...colors go in the trash as far as I know."

"I saw the garbage truck the other day...can you believe those guys who work right inside the back, sorting through all that shit by hand? Can only imagine what they come across in a day."

"They're probably immune to the germs...not like us gringos who catch every bug that's going around. There are worse jobs, I guess."

"I can't think of any off hand. Is that grill ready yet? I'm starving."

"Did Katie try that creole rub I gave her?"

"Not sure what she rubbed my meat with...but she is good at it."

We laughed. GP raised his glass. "Cheers to that."

Something scratched my leg. It was Coco, GP and Helen's long-haired Chihuahua. She had been abandoned by her owner, like many other canines in Melaque. Helen volunteered at a local animal shelter where they rescued dogs and tried to find people to adopt them. According to her, Coco was only with them temporarily but GP knew the little ankle biter would be going back to Canada with them in the spring.

Some expats lived at the resort full-time and others, like us, stayed part-time spending as much of the winter there as possible. Summers in Melaque were way too hot and humid for me. Katie and I spent the remainder of the year travelling elsewhere or just staying at home in Windsor. We paid the resort to reserve our apartment on an annual basis. Some opted to have it rented out to nationals while they were away during the summer months.

GP mentioned how much Katie loved Coco and she would be going home with us. I scoffed and reached down to pick up the little nipper. She was about the size of a squirrel, minus the tail. A Chihuahua and hamster mix, cute to every woman who saw her. I asked GP if he knew where Coco came from.

He wasn't sure, said they found her wandering around one of the beach restaurants. Someone thought she belonged to the cook but he disappeared around the same time she was found. He got her from a friend's litter near Coco Beach, thus the name.

"He disappeared or he got disappeared...like by the cartel?"

"Who knows? Maybe he was murdered...like that vegetable guy and the woman who owned the restaurant on the main drag, in Barra."

I rolled my eyes. "That would make three in less than two years...no wonder some of our friends back home think we're crazy coming to Mexico."

GP laughed. "Shit, when we lived in Atlanta it was an everyday occurrence...but it's so commonplace in the states it ain't news-worthy anymore. They save the headlines for mass-shootings with more impressive body counts."

Glasses of wine in hand, the women joined us. They handed over plates of meat for the grill. Helen scooped up Coco and rubbed her tiny head. Katie asked, "Who got killed now? You can't be talking about our little piece of paradise."

Helen spoke up. "Back when we lived in Atlanta..."

GP cut her off. "We already covered that, everyone knows the U.S. is the murder capital of the world and it will never change...they love their guns too much. Plenty of death and destruction to write about there, Ed."

I swallowed a mouthful of beer and stifled a burp. "Yeah, I know. Living and working across from Detroit and watching their daily news was always enlightening. Couldn't have paid me enough to be a cop there. Windsor's just fine, and I'm not too worried about little old Melaque...yet."

CHAPTER FIVE

Named

Amigo started his day before most people in Melaque. Somehow, he knew it wasn't his real name, but that's what everyone called him. It was a popular name. White people called the browns, Amigo. The browns called the whites Gringo. Both types of people were wasteful, leaving containers of leftover food outside their homes. Who was he to complain when it was so easy to find a free meal to start his day?

Finding suitable clothing proved more difficult since many places wanted money for the simplest of garments. Amigo wondered where it all came from and if he had more of his own somewhere, wherever he came from. He still couldn't remember but so much seemed familiar or easy to figure out, like the buildings in which people offered food or clothes in exchange for money.

Somehow, that stuff had to be earned so he waited until later in the day when visitors to the beach discarded their cans and bottles. They were worth money, something he needed to buy things people wouldn't give him for free. But Amigo learned making money wasn't as easy as he thought. It seemed simple enough when he watched another man collecting cans and trading them for money.

The other collector confronted him, claimed jurisdiction, and took all Amigo's cans. The man asked him who he thought he was and where he'd come from. Two questions that Amigo couldn't answer. It was another problem that perplexed him, his lack of speech. He thought he could speak at some point in his life but was at a loss as to why that had changed.

His first couple days were difficult in the seaside town called Melaque. After spending a miserable night on the beach, Amigo sought shelter in a thicket near the lagoon at what appeared to be an abandoned campsite. A tarp strung up between trees and an old mattress became his new home. There was also a fire pit but Amigo was unsure of why it would be needed in the tropical climate.

The previous occupant left a stack of bottles, like a picture window in his simple home. Amigo liked how the sun shone through the different colored receptacles in the morning. He stared through the glass kaleidoscope wondering what his previous home might have been like. That's when he came up with an idea on how to make some money to buy things everyone else seemed to take for granted.

CHAPTER SIX

The Bite Mark

Another party. It seemed that there was always some kind of celebration going on at our resort. Birthdays, anniversaries, and celebrations of life that happened way too often. On this occasion it was Fred's 70th birthday. He was a lumberjack in his previous life. His wife, Wilma, specialized in beer baking...something she did after being out drinking all evening. We called them the Flintstones because of the dune buggy they drove around town.

Fred was a big and burly guy with a heart of gold and bad hearing. Probably from the loud chainsaws buzzing in his ears all those years in the timberlands of British Colombia. BC was where most of the expats and visitors in Melaque came from. Being from Ontario, Katie and I were kind of a rarity.

We'd heard the sound of beer cans popping and mixers going the previous night so we knew Wilma would be treating us to something sweet at the birthday party. She managed a restaurant back home. But it was the meal I was looking forward to since Wilma brought both smoked and fresh BC Salmon just for the party.

Once awake, I peeked out the door. GP was already at one of the tables under the palapa pergola, with a beer in hand. It was happy hour, something that was announced by one of us ringing a little bell on the bar. Coco was always first to respond. Not like it was a mandatory thing, but when you're retired it's a way to socialize and do some day drinking.

GP played a 70's rock and roll play list on his portable speakers. I've never met a man who is more knowledgeable on the topic of music. He could win any trivia contest, I'm sure.

Named after the famous WWII tank commander, GP actually spent some time in giant armored vehicles while in the army. He worked in other professions too but he looked more like the kind of guy you'd see driving a tank. Think Telly Savalas in the movie *Kelly's Heroes*, minus the leather cap and cigar.

I announced to Katie happy happy was under way and GP was leading the charge as usual. She was busy preparing a salad for the party and said she'd meet us out there when she was done. Remembering I needed beer and ice, I headed out and asked GP if he needed anything at the corner store. He proudly displayed a fresh bottle of tequila in front of him and said, "Nope, bar fridge is full of beer.

And I hope Willy drinks that shitty Heineken I left in there...it's gone bad but he won't know the difference." He laughed out loud.

Willy and Wanda stayed a few blocks away and Katie asked if I could pick them up on the way to the store, they had food and booze to carry. They were waiting for me on the corner when I pulled up near their place, Big Willy already sweating like a pig, something we had in common.

"Long walk down the stairs to the street, eh buddy?"

Wanda dropped her cigarette and put it out with her sandal before they climbed into my car.

Willy answered. "We got no air up there and no breeze coming in today."

"I hear ya. Pool's nice today...those your swim trunks?"

"Why...we wearing them today? Don't you have a new sign that says no clothes in the pool?"

Wanda and I laughed. "I think they mean street clothes...after that bash last year where we all jumped in fully clothed. You need any ice? I gotta grab a bag at the store."

"Our beer bag is full but if you've got room in one of your coolers, I'll grab ice. We could use some smokes too."

By the time we got back to our table at the resort a few more people had gathered for happy hour. Party snacks were laid out so I stashed my beer in the cooler and went inside to retrieve my world-famous truffle cream cheese dip. It paired perfectly with beer or wine or any other beverage for that matter.

I grabbed a handful of Doritos before sitting down. They're so much cheesier in Mexico but contain jalapenos, like just about every-thing else in that country. I hate anything that burns my mouth but find them bearable with a cold beer to wash them down. GP dabbed a potato chip in the truffle dip and nodded his approval. Not that it was needed, I would have been happy to eat it all myself.

About a dozen of us were gathered when Bruce and Sticks showed up. Like the others, it wasn't his given name but his surname was Wayne so it was a no-brainer. GP wasted no time in announcing Batman's arrival. "Here he is...cancel the missing report."

Sticks was a few steps behind, as usual, and she didn't look im-pressed. Peppered with questions as to his whereabouts, Bruce only shrugged and said he wasn't sure what happened after he left the barbeque. He thought someone gave him Rohypnol, a roofie, and he woke up near the lagoon with a sore throat and no memory of how he got there.

"Ask him how he got the bite mark on his neck?" Sticks addressed the group. Bruce was wearing a collared Hawaiian shirt and doing his best to keep the mark hidden. His feisty friend pulled his shirt open to expose what appeared to be a fresh bruise, with impressions in the shape of a bite. "What's this look like to you?" She asked us. "He doesn't remember how he got it." Sticks walked around the table and sat beside Wanda.

I had to admit it surely looked like teeth impressions. GP asked, "Did you wander into the queer bar after you got roofied, Bruce? Maybe that's why your throat is sore."

Everyone laughed except the Batman. He only shrugged again and cracked a beer. In his defense, I suggested maybe he'd been abducted by aliens, like Doreen's cat. She swears it was taken and experimented on, after she witnessed strange lights in the sky over the mountain near Barra de Navidad. The woman rented bungalows near the beach and had a collection of rescue cats and dogs that actually looked like they'd been experimented on.

With a glass of wine in hand, Katie joined the group. "Are you talking about aliens again, Ed, you've been watching too many of those You Tube videos."

Her comment solicited a few more chuckles. Wanda, a retired nurse, made a show of examining Bruce for any other marks or clues as to where he might have disappeared to.

CHAPTER SEVEN

The Bottle Guy

Fred's birthday party took on a life of its own. It was a potluck affair with everyone bringing an appetizer and or salad. And besides the imported smoked and pink salmon, Wilma put out fresh-baked banana crème and apple pies. There was another party happening on the other side of the pool, some Quebecois that we didn't really hang out with at the resort.

Melaque attracted Canadians from across the country, with most snowbirds being from BC or Quebec. We also had a few people from the Prairie Provinces, and a handful of Americans. Basically, people who lived where it was cold and shitty in the winter. The Fenix de Melaque wasn't the cheapest place in town to stay but it was new and had all the amenities. Like a phoenix rising from the ashes, it was built on the ruins of the Hotel Casa Grande, once a world class resort devastated by an earthquake in 1995.

The conversation around our table got louder as the beer, wine and tequila took effect. The birthday boy, Fred, was the only abstainer in the group. Nobody ever asked him directly but he'd made comments in the past about having an intimate relationship with alcohol in his lumberjack days. The topic of Bruce's disappearance came up again, with more teasing and poking fun than any serious questions or inquiries.

Being the guest of honor, Fred sat at the head of the long table. Even with his hearing aids, it wasn't the best position for him to be included in conversation.

GP took a shot at Bruce. "I still think you stumbled into the queer bar and got roofied there."

Fred turned to me. "Bruce fell off the bar roof...which one?"

I tried not to laugh. It really wasn't funny and could be me someday. I was about to repeat what GP said to Bruce when Fred continued. "Is that why he was missing...was he unconscious or something?"

I didn't have the heart to correct him, and felt bad because I could tell he was struggling to hear what was going on. Fred said it was worse in crowds with all the background noise. Once a talented musician, his lack of hearing put an end to his band days. But the party was for him and he was a trouper, telling the odd joke or story that kept the laughter going.

Trying to steer the conversation away from himself, Bruce asked if anyone heard any more about the teacher and his dog, the pair who went missing on their morning walk. He said it happened close to where he woke up and found himself.

Big Willy said one of the crocs probably got them.

Fred turned to me wearing a silly grin. "What did Willy say about his cock?"

Out of common courtesy, I clued him in.

"Wilma and I have driven the buggy around that lagoon. There's lots of big crocodiles and some nasty-looking snakes in there. Wouldn't be the first dog to get snatched, but in all the years we've been coming here I don't know of anyone being eaten alive. Maybe if he was stupid enough to go in after the dog..."

Wanda spoke up. "He's not the first to go missing around here. What about the murders here and over in Barra? They can't all be cartel related. Why would they bother with simple folk in these small towns?"

I answered. "Who knows with those greedy bastards...remember the fake avocado and lime shortages they created to drive prices up? When I was in Puerto Vallarta, they controlled a lot of the beach vendors and taxi drivers."

Willy said, "No wonder Uber didn't try to make a go of it there...might see their heads hanging from an overpass."

Sticks gasped. Katie asked, "What about the woman who owned the restaurant in Barra. Why would anyone want to kill her?"

I replied. "Any number of reasons...and you can't always blame the cartel. Maybe she owed someone money or it was domestic related. Those are two of the most popular motives for murder."

Bruce addressed me. "Right up your alley, eh Ed?" Maybe you should write about what's going on...the murders in Melaque."

Big Willy chimed in. "Yeah, and we can all add our two cents...make it a group effort. We could form a club...like a murder club...where we decide who lives or dies. Maybe even solve these local crimes."

The gang laughed. Helen raised a glass and said, "Salud to the Melaque Murder Club."

A stranger appeared and started to collect our empty bottles. He looked familiar but I knew he wasn't a resort resident because we usually didn't let anyone else into the gated complex. I turned to Bruce and asked if he closed the gate when he came in or if he knew who the man was.

"That's the bottle guy, I think...from the beach. Someone must have let him in to collect our empties."

"Is he competing with the can guy?"

Bruce shrugged. Willy saw us eyeing the stranger. "Is that the guy from the beach?"

I responded. "Bruce says he's the bottle guy."

"Yeah, but isn't he the nude guy too?"

Katie overheard us. "It is...look at that scar on his neck...those five dots or whatever. I noticed that when he was on the beach."

I asked, "How the hell did you see that from a hundred yards away?"

She blushed slightly. "I used Willy's binoculars and saw everything close up."

I smiled. "I bet you did, Princess."

CHAPTER EIGHT

The Good, The Bad, and The Dead

A Melaque murder club? It was a novel idea, albeit hatched while consuming copious amounts of alcohol. As an author, I like having the power to decide who lives and who dies but sometimes it's a tough decision. You don't want to piss off your readers by killing off the protagonist or another character everyone likes.

I wrote Moon Mask, the sequel to one of my best sellers, Finding Hope. My youngest sister purchased the book—yes, I even charge family for my stories. How else can I support my travel habits? She said to me, "You better not have killed off Two Snakes in this book, I like him." Phew, dodged that bullet.

I sat in front of the laptop in my shady little spot on our patio, my retreat for creating and writing about the thirty-plus years I worked as a street cop and detective. There are so many stories to tell. When I retired nobody asked me to return my notebooks, which were property of the police service. Decades of names, most of whose faces I remembered, and every call or investigation I was ever involved in.

When I have my bookseller's hat on, I tell people names are changed to protect the guilty. Writing fiction has its advantages, protecting me legally, and allowing me to use my imagination to spice things up a bit to make a better story. Like they say in the movies, my stories are inspired by true events. I try to keep it real, and do my best to paint an accurate and vivid picture of what frontline policing is all about.

My Abigail Brown Crime Series is a bit different. The Detroit homicide detective was introduced in the first installment of Border City Chronicles, where her she and Norm Strom (my persona) meet through her uncle, a Detroit cop from my book Bloody Friday. Although I created Abigail in my own mind, her physical description and personality were pieced together by recalling some of the female cops I worked with over the years.

I have fun fictionalizing when writing about the Detroit homicide detective who investigates and specializes in serial killers. It's a popular sub-genre in the crime category, something that challenges me to be creative and keep my readers interested. Most of my fans are women...go figure. Too many men don't read, while their women are spending time alone with depraved criminals and cold-blooded killers.

Getting feedback from readers is paramount to me, whether good or bad. It's helped me mold my writing voice and fine tune what I call my retirement hobby. Gazing across the courtyard where distance blurred faces in the pool, I thought about the murder club. Maybe it would be a good muse...more fuel for my fire...brain food. A bunch of retirees sitting around trying to solve local murders with speculation, guesswork, and even rumors? That's funny.

Not that I wasn't interested in what was happening to people in our little Mexican beach town, but not knowing the victims made it less important. Were the occurrences connected or was there a story behind it? Something we could address at our first club meeting, if we ever actually had one. I chuckled to myself. Would we have weekly meetings as a group...another excuse for a party?

CHAPTER NINE

Bones

I was stretching, trying to get the kinks out, when I recognized the sound of the mayor's flip-flops coming down the stairs. Helen wasn't a mayor of anywhere, she earned the title mostly because she spoke a handful of languages fluently, and acted as our resort translator for any French or Spanish speaking people.

"Morning, Ed, did you see Facebook this morning?"

Part of my morning routine while waking up is checking my email and various social media accounts to see what's happening with family, friends and the rest of the world. "Yeah, I skimmed the notifications on my page. Why?"

"Did you see the post on the Friends of Melaque page...about the body they found in the lagoon? Do you think it's the teacher and his dog?"

"Didn't see that...could be, I guess. Probably not the only body in that swamp."

"Are you going for your walk? Mind if I tag along today?"

I swung my arms up, cracking both shoulders, and twisted my neck from side to side. It sounded like elastic bands snapping. "Sure, do you need to change your shoes first?"

"Geez, does that hurt? Sounds like Rice Krispies." She glanced down at her feet. "Yeah, these won't work...give me a minute." Helen turned and headed back up the stairs.

GP bellowed from their balcony, above. "Hey copper, you going to check out the body in the lagoon?"

I hadn't considered it but had to admit I was curious. "Can't hurt to stroll down that way and see what's going on...big news for our little hamlet." I heard Helen coming back down the stairs and addressed GP. "Tell the mayor I'll be back in a second...gotta get something in the apartment."

He nodded and blew smoke rings over the railing of his balcony, as if he was playing a ring toss game, trying to lasso the small palm tree below. I called up to him as Helen joined me. "Your talents never cease to amaze me, sir."

The mayor glanced up at her husband and back to me. "You ready? Maybe we can walk to the lagoon and see what's going on."

"Great minds think alike."

The walk to the lagoon was a bit further than I usually went on my daily route. Melaque is actually an amalgamation of three smaller towns...all fishing villages at one time...Villa Obregon on the east end, San Patricio in the middle, and Melaque on the west side. The town stretches for a little over a mile along one of the many bays in the Pacific, along what's called the Costalegre.

We followed the roads paralleling the beach until we found the path that skirted the west side of the lagoon. All was quiet and the mayor said the social media post was probably just fake news. Following the path north, I saw two small boats in the lagoon near the shoreline. They slowly paddled their way through the floating masses of water flora.

Rounding the next corner, we saw several men, some in uniform, gathered near the water's edge on the malecon. Not being familiar with how they handled missing persons or recovered bodies in Mexico, I scanned the gathering trying to figure out who the various investigators were. I recognized two uniformed men as the National Guard, an organization that now encompasses what used to be the Federals, or Federal Police. There were three more men in military camo-type uniforms, possibly State Police or the Marines who patrolled the towns along the sea.

Other men were in casual attire, including the men in boats who who appeared to be locals using their own watercraft. They worked with long poles and dragnets, trolling the area for what I assumed was either evidence or more body parts. It was doubtful they were searching for a dog. There was no yellow crime scene tape like we use at home, but one of the uniformed soldiers moved to stop our approach.

He spoke to us in Spanish. I was only able to decipher a couple of words...stop, no entry, and go away. This was the mayor's area of expertise and she conversed with the man in his native tongue. While he was distracted by her, I pulled out my wallet that I'd retrieved it before leaving the apartment.

I had retained my police detective badge and flashed it just long enough for him to see, hoping he didn't notice my finger covering the part that said, Retired. The soldier seemed confused by this and whatever other line of crap Helen fed him. I stepped around the two of them and moved closer to see what was going on. Bones were visible, wet and glistening, tinted yellow by the morning sunlight.

A human skeleton was laid out on a blue tarp, covering the paved malecon. A man was down on one knee examining the bones and another took pictures with his mobile phone. During my policing career I saw many bodies but only a few skeletal remains. Used to seeing mutilated or burnt flesh on mostly fresh corpses, I found it odd the bones were completely bare.

One of the other soldiers, a man wearing stripes on his shoulder, shouted at his comrade talking to Helen. Before I could get any closer, he grabbed me from behind and tugged on my arm to pull me away from the scene. He and his supervisor exchanged words in Spanish that didn't sound very nice. The mayor told me it was time to go. They were threatening to arrest us if we didn't leave immediately.

The mayor and I walked back the way we came and talked about what we saw. Getting back on the main road she stopped and turned to face me. "I think it's time to call a meeting of the Murder Club."

CHAPTER TEN

The Club

The walk back to our resort seemed to go quicker than the walk to the lagoon. As if injected with adrenaline, Helen's words flew out of her mouth like bullets fired from a machine gun. She had ideas and theories but more questions than answers. I could tell it was a new experience for her and she was a bit freaked out. Me, not so much. Sarcastically, my wife called me Mister Excitement. Been there, seen that.

I had witnessed all sorts of human carnage as a police officer: shootings, stabbings, car accidents and fights, resulting in everything from minor flesh wounds to decapitations. Even though I had been retired for over a decade, I was still infected with a common affliction. Human curiosity.

I was a problem solver, the type of person who liked answers to the unexplained. But I'm not a 'why' guy and I don't need a reason for everything. Sometimes shit just happens. You can't always explain the stupid or violent things one human being maliciously does to another. They might be a psychopath or simply do it for fun. The world is full of crazy people.

The mayor was ready to explode and spill her guts when we burst through the gate at our resort but no one was there. Katie left a note saying she and GP took their bikes down to the market to pick up a few things. The weekly event was set up close to the lagoon and they could have met the mayor and I, but obviously they weren't the curious cats we were.

We saw the Flintstones cruising through town on their way to do some off-roading somewhere. Willy, Wanda, Bruce and Sticks would probably be at the beach table later in the day, so I figured on waiting until then to call the murder club to order. Day drinking in the hot sun was the perfect place to solve all the world's problems.

Finally, Lolita emerged from the laundry room carrying an arm load of bed linen. She worked for the resort and provided us maid service once a week. I thought she was going to have a heart attack when Helen unloaded on her. She crossed herself at least five times while hearing the gory tale. The two women babbled on in Spanish.

I peeled off my shirt and jumped into the pool. After lowering my body temperature enough to stop sweating, I retired to our apartment and gathered up some fixings for breakfast. A bacon and fried egg sandwich were on the menu and I went to work prepping my meal. They say that breakfast is the most important meal of the day. For me, I could eat bacon and eggs at any meal. On occasion, Katie made us a quiche or omelet for dinner.

By the time she got back I was on the patio, writing. Abigail Brown was busy putting the pieces of her serial killer puzzle together. My wife requested my assistance in unloading the two carriers on her bike so I paused mid-sentence, holding on to my thoughts. They were lost when she asked me what was going on at the lagoon. The market was buzzing with news of a gruesome discovery.

She asked what I thought, as a retired police investigator. I explained how I bluffed my way into the area for a closer look, and how Helen and I were almost arrested., but I admitted I had no ideas. As if proud of me for accomplishing something important, Katie kissed me on the cheek and said she couldn't wait to tell the others at the beach.

The usual characters were already at the beach table when we got there. I was immediately attacked by a flurry of questions as to why I was there twice in one week. I told everyone I missed them, but they knew better. Sticks asked if we saw the viral post on Facebook about the body discovered in the lagoon. The conversation exploded from there, leaving me no chance to call the club meeting to order.

I let the discussion run a few minutes before using my cop voice —that's what Katie called it—to get everyone's attention. Having sat on boards and committees of clubs and associations in the past, I explained the rules of decorum.

Big Willy cut me short and asked if the mayor shouldn't be running things, like she did at the resort.

I suggested our sheriff, Katie, be in charge of our murder club. She earned the title one day when the mayor wasn't around and some French tourists invited themselves into our resort to look around. They went so far as to ask for a glass of wine and what I was cooking on the barbeque for dinner. When I asked Katie if she knew who the strangers were, she went ballistic and told them they were trespassing.

It was the reason we had to keep the gate locked. Without making an appointment or attempt to contact resort management, tourists were always trying to look over the gate or sneak in to see what was hiding behind our walls. She might be small, but my wife is mighty and she chased the interlopers off the property. They left with their tails between their legs, scared off by the new sheriff in town.

The others at the beach table agreed Katie was a good choice to be club president. She told everyone how she was secretary of our HOA back home but she was underqualified and a bit nervous taking on her new role. Bruce said I could be her consigliere and advise her on matters concerning police procedures and associated legal matters. Willy seconded the motion but admitted he had no idea what Bruce just said.

Things had just settled down and we were each taking turns sharing what we knew about the discovery in the lagoon, when Tequila Tommy showed up. He lived in the same city back home as Willy and Wanda, and had been friends with them for years. Tommy was a small man with a big thirst for beer and tequila, thus the handle. He plopped his cooler bag on the table and grabbed a chair.

"Hey, did you guys here about the bodies they found in the lagoon?"

"Bodies, plural?" I asked. Had more been discovered or was the story growing?

"That's what I heard at the barbershop this morning...two gay guys from Villa Obregon, and their dog."

Separate conversations broke out around the table. "I don't know who the bones belonged to but the mayor and I saw one set of skeletal remains laid out on the malecon, not too far from the beach."

Sticks spoke up. "Bruce, isn't that where you said you woke up after you disappeared for the night?"

Tommy swallowed a gulp of beer. "What? When did this happen...what did I miss?"

Bruce got up. "I'm going for a pee." He headed for the ocean, the cleanest toilet in town.

Wanda answered Tommy. "After the steak barbeque...Bruce never made it home and woke up near the lagoon. He doesn't know how he got there and thinks someone drugged him."

We all laughed, Tommy the hardest. "That's a good one. Oh, sorry Sticks...I'm sure there's some truth to it...that he drank too much and made a wrong turn on the way home. Funny though, how you only live two blocks from the resort. Anyway, what have you guys heard about the lagoon thing?"

Everybody started talking at once, again. Tommy turned his head from person to person, as if he was playing whack-a-mole and didn't know which one to hit. He heard someone say something about our new venture. "A murder club? Count me in."

CHAPTER ELEVEN

Assignments

GP and Helen weren't at the beach table, they'd gone off to spend the day with some friends who were visiting from back home. Everyone else was still gabbing, throwing around names of the missing and murdered and offering suggestions on how our club could get involved to answer some questions. No one expected to hear anything from the police, who were stationed miles down the road, in the larger City of Cihuatlan.

Katie suggested we all have assignments and asked for my advice on what we needed to do. Considering my previous life and investigative experience, I gave specific jobs to each person around the table. I told Tommy to poke around the barber shop again for updates, and get the latest gossip from the different bars he frequented.

Wanda asked what she could do. Since she was familiar with many of the beach vendors, I suggested she question them to see if they knew anything. Seeing that Willy was anxiously awaiting his assignment I said he could act as his wife's bodyguard in case someone didn't like her line of questioning. I also told him to talk to the neighbors in their building.

Sticks offered to check with Trudi and Rudi, the town gossips. They knew everything about whatever everyone else in town was doing. They were like a local encyclopedia for everything from current events to juicy gossip.

Bruce was well-read and an excellent researcher so I suggested he do just that and scour information sources like news and social media sites.

The Flintstones weren't present but I said they could reach out to all the different friends they had in town, locals and expats alike. GP and Helen weren't there either but it was obvious she'd be our official interpreter if and when we had to question the locals. I asked the group what we should have GP do and Tommy suggested he supply tequila for the meetings.

Besides being club president, Katie asked what she could do. I thought for a second then suggested she question the vendors she knew at the market. They met hundreds of people on a daily basis and surely picked up on the scuttlebutt when they were in town.

Everyone knew about my job in a former life and Bruce asked what my role would be in all of this. Not knowing exactly how suspicious deaths were handled locally or in Mexico, I offered to do my own research on exactly how they handled such things. I couldn't think of anyone I knew in local or federal policing, but there was a retired RCMP and an L.A. cop staying in town. Everyone knew someone in Melaque so I thought they could be a place to start.

Big Willy wanted to hear firsthand what the mayor and I saw at the lagoon. They'd already heard most of the story but I went into more detail. I said how I was surprised at the lack of clothing or flesh on the skeleton.

Sticks reacted by scrunching her face and shaking her head. They heard how the bones looked pristine, as if they'd been boiled and polished, and how I was able to see scrape marks on one of the femurs."

Bruce inquired, "You mean like teeth marks? Crocodiles could surely do that."

"I'm no expert, Bruce, but I don't think so. From what I've read and seen on the tube, they like to drag their prey down to the bottom and tenderize the meat before they have dinner. The skeleton we saw appeared intact...you would think crocs would tear it apart...especially if more than one shared the meal or they fought over it. Have any of you seen them feed the crocodiles over in La Manzanilla? They throw them hunks of chicken...it's crazy."

Sticks continued making faces, looking disgusted, as if she was about to be sick. "What about Bruce's bite mark...do you think a crocodile did this?" She pulled his collar back to expose the mark. Its appearance had changed and looked like blisters or a scar of sorts.

I leaned over the table for a closer look. "Doesn't look like a crocodile bite to me but what do I know? Weird...it kinda looks like one of those raised tattoos or what they call scarring that some people do to decorate their skin."

Sticks heard me but I could tell she wasn't happy with the answer. She snapped at him. "Do you remember going to a tattoo parlor, Bruce?"

Tommy asked if the meeting was over. He was late for his next pit stop.

Katie looked to me for approval, and told him he was dismissed.

I thought we might discuss the other missing and murdered people in town but Katie and Wanda said they had to pee. I let it be and they headed for the ocean.

Sticks called out and told them to wait up, she wanted to go for a swim.

Bruce told her to stay out of the warm water near the other women.

The bottle guy appeared at our table and pointed to some emp-ties in the sand. Willy greeted the man. "Hola, Amigo, go ahead." The man smiled and bent down to retrieve our discarded bottles.

I noticed the strange mark on his neck, almost identical to the one Bruce had. Big Willy saw it too. He turned and looked at me. We wondered the same thing and stared at Bruce. He stared back. "What?"

CHAPTER TWELVE

The Bridge

I stuck to my usual routine the next morning. Waking up in front of the laptop, followed by a few stretches and a walk. What wasn't routine was the route I took. Needing a change of scenery each day, I decided to head west to check out the new bridge they were building. The span would allow pedestrians to keep their feet dry while crossing the river that separated Melaque from the new multi-million-dollar malecon on the other side.

Only in Mexico, would they build a beautiful walkway that was not directly accessible from town. There had been some kind of bridge there in the past but it was washed away by one of the annual summer floods. While construction was under way, we had to walk north to the edge of town and a short distance down the highway, before taking a dirt road back south to get to the malecon.

The extra walk was good for exercise but basically a pain in the ass. The river was shallow and narrow enough most people just trudged through it or got their feet wet crossing over. The malecon had recently been beautified and redone, making for a nice place to stroll alongside the mountain that protected the west end of Melaque.

It was under a kilometer in length and offered a panoramic view of the beach and coastline all the way to Barra de Navidad. Waves crashing on the rocks below and the odd fisherman trying to catch a meal, made for a lovely morning stroll. The only downside was the oncoming heat from the rising sun. Any breeze in town came out of the west and was, unfortunately blocked by the serious rock wall that rose above the malecon.

I always carried a camera on my morning walks, capturing images of unique doors or whatever else caught my attention. Today my mind was elsewhere, playing scenarios of abductions and murder. Whether it was my cop-mind or simple human curiosity, I couldn't stop myself from thinking about the strange occurrences in our quiet little town.

After checking on the snail-paced construction of the new bridge, I made a U-turn and was about to head up a side street when I saw Julio. He owned a local watering hole of the same name, and was sweeping the sidewalk out front. I offered my best Spanglish. "Buenos Dias, Julio, como estas?"

"Buenos Dias, Ed...I'm good...you?" He knew I had pretty well depleted my collection of Spanish words. "Where'd jew walk dis morning?"

"I was hoping to cross the new bridge and do the malecon but it doesn't look like it that bridge will be done anytime soon."

Julio laughed. Si, the governor was here yesterday for the unveiling of the bridge and new malecon but...it's Mexico...jew know?"

"Si, amigo, I know very well. How's business lately...I hear you're running the bar next door now too?"

"Si. My way of...how you say...eliminating competition? I can't keep up but it's better den someone else making de money."

I shuffled sideways, trying to make my exit, and avoid a long conversation but Julio continued. "Jew hear about de guy day found in the lagoon? Nutting but bones day say." He held the broom in one hand and crossed himself with the other.

"Yeah, we heard...you know anything about it?"

"No. Only he was a gringo...and day will have to investigate...that would not happen if he was Mexican. Nobody would care."

I was back-stepping and creating distance. "I hear you, amigo, we'll see you for drinks and dinner soon."

Already turned around and heading in the opposite direction, Julio called out to me. "Say hello to jor lovely wife for me."

Picking up the pace, I pulled out my sweat towel and wiped my face. The heat and humidity were already working on me and I wasn't even half-way into my walk. Being a sweat hog, I complained about the humidity back home and in Melaque.

The pool called my name the moment I walked through the gate and into our resort. The pool guy and groundskeeper always got a kick out of watching me take my morning plunge. They would always laugh and say something about how cold the water was, that it was only suitable for polar bears and Canadians. These were the same people you saw wearing parkas when the mercury dipped below 80 degrees Fahrenheit.

GP heard my splash and called down from his balcony. "How's the water, Ed?"

"Not bad once you break through the ice."

He laughed. "Hey, we gonna go to Las Hamacas for happy hour later...the Bandito's are playing?"

"I'll have to talk to my social director but I'm sure she won't need any coaxing. Where's the mayor this morning? I didn't run across her during my walk." I climbed out of the pool and grabbed my towel.

"She's working at the animal shelter today so I'm dog-sitting. Any news from our club members?" He clucked. "As if you're ever going to find the truth about any of it...the Mexican government is worse than ours and even more corrupt."

"I haven't heard anything but have an idea for after happy hour...a little adventure."

"Do tell, detective..."

"You'll see..."

CHAPTER THIRTEEN

Field Trip

Any conversation about murder at our table was drowned out by the Banditos. True to their name, they resemble a mix of ZZ Top and Poncho Villa. They're scary-looking kind of dudes you'd clear a path for, even in broad daylight. The lead guitarist had long black hair swaying back and forth across his dark sunglasses. A cigarette hung from his lower lip and a cloud of smoke added to the effect.

But their looks were deceiving. They were the nicest guys you could ever meet and they even played for charity, on this occasion,...raising money for a local's medical bills. I was more than impressed when they played tunes from bands like Procol Harum and King Crimson...stuff you'd never hear on the radio.

Many of the town's restaurants offered live entertainment to grab their share of business from snowbird seniors trying to relive their younger days with booze and music. Rock wasn't the only genre you could find in town. There were duets, jazz, and Spanish guitar music. Some artists started early in the afternoon at one venue and continued playing somewhere else in town, until us old folks were tucked in for the night.

The Banditos played a couple sets, finishing around 6pm. Everyone one at our table had a few drinks and something to eat before we watched the band pack up to move on. The murder topic got lost somewhere during the toe-tapping and singing along. Katie suggested we check out the sunset down at Twiggs, a bar completely constructed out of driftwood collected from area beaches. That included the restrooms.

I fetched the Impala and six of us squeezed into five seats, something we usually did after a late night out, instead of having to call a taxi. The grunting, groaning, and occasional groping was always more fun when everyone had a glow on. Except for me, the driver. Not that it mattered in Melaque, the chances of getting pulled over were about the same as winning a multi-million-dollar lottery.

We took turns capturing images of each other with the setting sun in the background. At the east end of the beach and from that angle, the sun set on the water instead of behind the mountain. It was always cool to watch the sky, changing to unimaginable colors as our world brought on the night. My favorite joke was telling everyone to listen carefully so they could hear the hissing sound of the sun hitting the water.

Twiggs bar is sandwiched between the ocean and lagoon. The skeletal remains, and missing person they belonged to, never left my mind. I held off earlier in the evening but it was time to announce my fieldtrip. Half the group eyed me like I had two heads when I suggested visiting the spot where the mayor and I saw the bones. Willy, Wanda, Helen and Katie said they were in. GP said his back had enough for one day so he volunteered to drive the other chicken's home.

It was only a short drive to the nearest entrance for the lagoon malecon. The sky was a virtual rainbow, with the darkest indigoes over our end of town and hues of burnt orange on the west side. We had to hurry while there was still enough daylight to find our way and avoid alerting any mosquitoes to our presence.

Being fast-walkers, the mayor and the sheriff led the way. Plagued by various ailments and nagging old injuries, Willy, Wanda and I brought up the rear. Helen paused and asked if we were there yet. I said it was a bit further, near the red brick wall at the back of the condominium building. Katie switched on her phone light to avoid tripping in holes. Paving stones were missing from the pathway or concealed by evening shadows.

I knew all evidence of what Helen and I had seen before would be gone but felt the others should get a feel for the place, kind of like sneaking around a graveyard at night. A sound in the water brought us all to a halt. We didn't need the flashlight to see what it was. Two burning amber spheres stared back at us. Was it something alien?

Wanda gasped and Katie clutched my arm so tight she nearly cut off the circulation. Helen asked if it was a crocodile.

I'd read about their nocturnal habits and heard something about their evil eyes but never witnessed it personally. Mesmerized, none of us moved.

Big Willy said, "Holy shit, do you see that?"

I replied. "Yeah...look at that monster..."

"Not just him, Edmundo, look around...further out in the lagoon."

I couldn't believe what was out there. It was if a hundred Chinese lanterns had settled on top of the water. The surface was perfectly calm and like a giant pool of black ink. There were too many eyes to count and they all seemed to be watching us. No doubt at least one of us peed a bit when we heard a commotion in the reeds.

Sounds of splashing and the fluttering of wings left us all speech-less. I caught a glimpse of white, reflected by the light of a partial moon. A snowy egret took to the sky. We were all backtracking at that point.

Katie said, "Let's get the hell out of here."

As we turned to leave, my peripheral vision caught something else white, sticking out of the reeds where the bird had been. "Look at that...it's someone's arm."

CHAPTER FOURTEEN

Doctor's Appointment

First thing the next morning, I packed up a box of books and headed for one of the local restaurants where they were hosting an artisan market. I was invited to join other local vendors who sold everything from fresh baked goods to fine Mexican art. Having sold some of my books to fellow snowbirds in the past, I decided to try my luck at the market.

I took the car since I had books to carry. On the way, I saw the police were in town and thought about telling them what we'd seen the previous night. With my obvious language barrier, I wasn't sure how I would do that without tying up my whole day trying to explain and show them our discovery? Being almost sure that someone else would see and report it, I continued on to the market.

There were about a dozen vendors, set up in a horseshoe on the dancefloor at the bar/restaurant. At these types of events, my table always ended up right next to the goodies—cookies, butter tarts, banana bread, and other carb-killers that weren't on my diet. Everyone swore by the cabbage rolls and people were already lining up so I grabbed some while they were still available.

Turns out the retired Canadians who made all the goodies were also readers so we took advantage of some bartering. My books sold well for a small market but Melaque is loaded with seniors who love to read and are always looking for something new. Dr. Lee had a table across from me, where he was accepting charitable donations for a local family's medical bills. He was also the owner of the restaurant.

The good doctor was retired from his medical practice and local politics, and was the well-respected, self-appointed historical expert on the area. He was also a decent musician. I'd met Lee several times during our stays in Melaque, mostly when we rented an apartment owned by his ex-wife. He came over to my table to discuss my books and expressed his own interest in putting something together covering the town's history.

After hearing him out, I asked him if he knew anything about the missing people in the area and the bones found in the lagoon.

Dr. Lee was a soft spoken gentle man. He offered a smile, paused in thought for a moment, then pulled up a chair to my table. "You're the retired policeman, correct?"

"Yes, sir." I returned the smile." I guess you can say I have a natural curiosity for such things but everyone in town is concerned with what's been going on over the last year or so."

He held the happy expression for another moment. "You know I'm retired too and am not involved in those kinds of things anymore. That is privileged information that I'm not privy to, being out of the loop, so to speak."

Having lost my shade, I wiped sweat from my brow.

The doctor continued. "Having said that, I still have connections and do hear things...people trust me and tell me stuff even when I wish not to hear it." He took a deep breath and sighed. "Yes, bad things have been happening lately in our town but it's not the norm. Maybe just a few bad apples...you know what I mean?"

"For sure, it's the same everywhere."

"I know the people you ask about, some personally, like Maria from Barra. You may not have heard anything but we have a way of taking care of our own in Melaque. No one was arrested for her murder but that doesn't mean that the person responsible hasn't paid a price. And Pablo, the man who ran the vegetable market...that was out of our hands. The cartels don't operate here, per say, but bad things can still happen when you cross the wrong people."

I knew exactly what Lee was talking about when he said they took care of their own. The first year we stayed in Melaque, another snowbird had her purse stolen from their bungalow when she went to bed and left the patio door open to catch the breeze. Locals spread the word and her purse was returned two days later with only a few dollars missing. Our landlord told us the police weren't involved, but the thief was caught and dealt with.

The doctor told me he played bridge with a group of friends in the medical profession, one of whom is the current medical examiner for the Cihuatlan area. His friend unofficially briefed the group about the recovered skeletal remains discovered in the lagoon because of the unusual condition they were found in. He said the flesh appeared to have been surgically removed and the bones were brittle, as if boiled in bleach.

The confused expression on Lee's face made me think he was trying to come up with his own hypothesis for the gruesome discovery. I thought about what we saw the previous night on our field trip and almost let it slip, but decided against it. For good measure, I inquired if crocodiles might be responsible for such carnage.

The doctor smiled again. "Not unless they know how to use a scalpel."

CHAPTER FIFTEEN

Club Agenda

I had time for a nap after the Sunday market and awoke to see the gang had started happy hour without me. They were discussing the murder club and our little field trip the night before. Mixed feelings were expressed. Some members weren't thrilled about being scared shitless and running home. Katie was not impressed with our discovery, and a bit more vocal than I expected. Sticks shook her head through the whole conversation, glad she wasn't there.

Willy and Wanda thought it was cool, kind of like checking out neighborhood displays on Halloween night. Finally, the mayor spoke up and said we should have reported it to the police. That started a heated debate with varying opinions on the level of confidence in Mexican authorities.

Fred tilted his head to Wilma and asked what everyone was arguing about. She told him it was about the bones we saw on our field trip.

"They saw Ed's bone?"

Bruce and Sticks laughed out loud but not everyone heard Fred. Wilma looked into his ear. "Put your damn hearing aids in."

He shrugged and leaned in closer trying to hear more about my appendage.

Wilma said they talked to some of their friends, locals who knew the woman in Barra very well. The word on the street was her death was domestic related, that Maria was serving more than food in her restaurant and having an affair with someone else's husband. And according to the rumor, the aggrieved spouse's brother was connected to one of the cartels.

Sticks asked if anyone heard more about the retired teacher and his dog. I jumped in and told the group about my conversation with the doctor. Fred asked if it was because of my bone and did I take too much Viagra. Laughter erupted and GP called for a toast to my boner. He lined up shot glasses and poured tequila.

Using the drink to clear my throat, I filled the club in about my conversation with Lee. "The doc said authorities haven't identified who the bones belonged to yet but there were strange striations or cut marks where the flesh may have been removed with a medical instrument."

Big Willy asked, "They sure it wasn't crocs...I couldn't believe how many we saw in the lagoon last night." He turned to Bruce. "You ever see how their eyes glow in the dark?"

"I've read about it but can't say I've ever seen it...I don't make a habit of being anywhere near that lagoon at night."

Sticks spoke up. "Yeah, only once but you can't remember."

I thought about the strange marks on Batman's neck and wondered if Willy ever asked him about it. Thinking it wasn't the right time to put Bruce on the spot, I told the others the doctor didn't have much else to say but he would reach out to some of his connections and try to gain more information.

The more we learned about the missing and murdered, the heavier our conversation grew. I could tell that not everyone was impressed with trying to figure out things for ourselves. Once again, the mayor suggested we get the police involved and that maybe Don, the retired Mountie who might have connections.

GP waived her off. "He's retired and no more help than Ed, honey. No offense, big guy."

I shrugged. "None taken. GP's right, Helen, we've both been out of the game for years and we have no clout here in Mexico."

"But you still have your badge..."

"They don't care about that...could be from a box of Cracker Jacks for all they care. Although it got me out of a jamb in Puerto Vallarta one time."

GP chuckled. "Do tell, copper."

Checking Katie's expression, I shook my head. "Maybe some other time. Perhaps we can call a vote to see if we should continue pursuing answers about the missing and murdered."

The others agreed. Fred asked Wilma what we were voting on.

"They want to know if you want to continue the club."

"A club sandwich would be good, thanks honey."

We laughed and most raised their hands to continue our quest. Katie wasn't sure but wanted to be a team player. The mayor abstained. The motion carried, which meant another round of shots.

CHAPTER SIXTEEN

Twins

Melaque seemed like a nice place to live. There was an ache deep in his belly that he couldn't explain. A longing or yearning for his true home? Amigo learned to adapt to his new surroundings. At least he assumed they were new because he couldn't remember where he came from or why he was there.

Certain people in town still gave him strange looks and seemed uncomfortable around him. For the most part, he got along and was accepted into their society. The folks at the Fenix were particularly generous, allowing him into the gated complex to collect their discarded bottles. And they had a lot of them, so much so that Amigo had to fix up an old cart to haul them away. Those gringos drank a lot of beer and tequila.

Sometimes he'd linger and eavesdrop on conversations to learn more about people, perhaps shedding some light on himself. Maybe something would jog his memory or help bring it back. They seemed to understand he couldn't speak and were kind enough to only ask him questions he could answer with a nod or shake of his head. That was the extent of his sign language.

Bruce took an interest and spent time with Amigo. He asked questions that might help him remember his past life. Amigo felt a connection to the man they called Batman, especially after seeing the mark on his neck similar to his own. He discovered it in a bathroom mirror one day.

Bruce was swimming at the Fenix when Amigo noticed it. Afraid to ask or say anything, he waited for a private conversation to point it out. The gringo went through his usual routine, questioning him about his childhood, trying to spark a memory. Recalling nothing new, Amigo pulled down the neckline on his shirt.

Bruce stared, appearing shocked at first. Muscles in his face twitched, then relaxed, growing expressions of confusion and curiosity. He reached out to touch Amigo's neck but he pulled back. Amigo reciprocated and pointed at the gringo's neck. Bruce exposed his mark and the two men touched each other at the same time.

The flesh was raised, leaving bumps or protrusions like small welts or skin tags. Five on each of them, in a wide V shape, like a set of five pins in bowling. Bruce felt a light surge of electricity run through his fingertips and up his arm. His eyes locked onto Amigo's. "Did you feel that too?"

Amigo nodded. A curtain of silence fell between them for a minute while they took each other in and tried to comprehend what just happened. Bruce was a well-read and intelligent man, but he was at a loss for words or an explanation. He had questions for the stranger but knew he couldn't get the detailed responses he desired. Then he had an idea.

The Batman turned to an empty page of the crossword book he'd been working on and wrote a question to Amigo. He turned the book around to see if the man could read it. Without hesitation, Amigo took the pen from Bruce and wrote an answer. It said, 'Yes, I can read...and apparently write but I don't know how or why."

It was a great breakthrough. They continued with short ques-tions and answers but other than proving Amigo could read and write, the exchange didn't shed any light on what both men really wanted to know. Bruce conveyed to Amigo he had some throat pain and was hoarse for a day but his speech wasn't affected. So, why did they both have the same marks and how did they get them?

CHAPTER SEVENTEEN

The 12th Hole

Gary Hart loved golf. Whether at home or while travelling, he always had his clubs with him. To Gary, a par golfer at best, it was all about getting out on a beautiful sunny day with his buddies to drink beer and chase a little white ball across manicured green turf. What could be better? Not the weather, it was always eighty-five and sunny at the Grand Bay golf resort on Isla de Navidad.

He and Brad Giroux had seasonal memberships there, allowing them to golf just about anytime they wanted, except on certain occasions when the club catered to the rich and shameless. It wasn't the best of courses, especially on the last section of twenty-seven holes, where the owners had let things go. Rumor was the family patriarch died and his kids were fighting over which possessions they wanted to keep.

That crap had nothing to do with Gary. His extended family was freezing their asses off in Saskatoon, while he and his wife basked in the warmth of their Mexican winter home. They'd fallen in love with Melaque years earlier and bought their own place in which to live out their golden years. Snow, ice, and gloomy skies were only shitty memories.

Big Willy and Tequila Tommy joined Brad and Gary for the two for one golf special, allowing the two non-members access to the course for the day. The men all knew each other from years of overwintering in Melaque. They golfed together when Gary and Brad were able to share their membership privileges.

Gary was normally the better golfer in the group, until the beer kicked in and he lost his swing. Brad knew this and tried to take advantage by betting more on the later holes. Even with the special, the course was quiet on this occasion. The hot and humid weather never seemed to be a factor with attendance. The slow day was more likely due to the annual sailing regatta at the marina, part of the Grand Bay Resort complex.

The foursome knocked off the front nine in record time. Dry conditions and hard turf added yards to their drives on the fairway. The greens weren't much better but putting was Gary's strong point. He had a nice glow on after pounding three beers and a hot dog at the turn. He fought to control his swing, teeing off on the tenth hole. Tommy caught up to him by number eleven.

Trying to take his lead back, Gary over shot the green on twelve. His ball disappeared over the lip and headed for the ocean. Knowing the sand would stop the ball dead, he wasn't too worried. Being furthest from the hole, Gary went off in search of his ball. Ocean waves crashed onto the beach about a hundred yards away.

He stood there for a moment, in awe of the pristine shoreline that ran for miles in either direction. His ball was nowhere in sight so he searched the rough to the right. Brad hollered for him to get his ass back in the game. Gary heard rustling in the thicket and saw movement. 'Great,' he thought, 'some critter's got hold of my ball'.

He used his golf club to move the bushes aside. Brad called out again but Gary never answered.

CHAPTER EIGHTEEN

Gone, Golfing

Big Willy and Tequila Tommy stumbled into the resort, charging at our table like injured bulls at an anxious Matador. The rest of the Murder Club was having a quiet pot-luck dinner. Like they were in a race to see who could spew the most words in a minute, both men blurted out their story at the same time. As if watching a pie-eating contest, we snapped our heads back and forth, waiting to see who would finish first.

Tommy succumbed. He reached for a tequila bottle on the table and didn't bother to use a shot glass. Willy stopped and gasped for air. "Anyone got a beer? Tommy, gimme that bottle when you're done."

From what we'd gathered during their tirade, the men lost Gary Hart while they were golfing. Most of us knew the man, he was staying with a friend of ours who lived in Melaque year-round. I couldn't stand the suspense. "How, exactly, did you lose Gary?"

Big Willy was busy downing a beer, something he probably didn't need, judging by his wobble. Tommy answered. "We didn't lose him, Ed, he disappeared on the twelfth hole at the golf course."

At least three of us answered at the same time. "What?"

Willy came up for air. "He over-shot the green and went to search for his ball. We called out because he was taking so long but he never answered. Brad went over the hill to find him but he was gone. Vanished."

GP asked, "How could he just disappear in the middle of the golf course?"

Tommy replied, "We don't know...thought maybe he drowned or something but the ocean isn't that close to the green...and then we saw his club and one shoe..."

Fred spoke up "So, is it Gary or his club that's missing and why do we need a gumshoe to find them?"

We considered his statement for a nanosecond. The mayor asked, "So, where's Brad, did you lose him too?"

They both answered. "No."

Big Willy continued, "He's still there, talking to the authorities...we searched all over and so did the groundskeepers. They called the cops...or whoever. We left before they came...you know how they blame us gringos for everything. They'll think we got drunk and did something stupid."

Wilma spoke up. "Well, did you?"

They both shook their heads. Tommy took another pull off the half-empty bottle of tequila.

Katie said, "This is crazy...people murdered and missing, bones in the lagoon, and now someone we know?"

I asked Big Willy, "Any crocodiles on the course? Maybe one grabbed him and dragged him off somewhere?"

"I've seen them at the run-down section, in the retention pond, but not anywhere near the twelfth hole...it's all beach around there. We thought about that too but the grounds keeper says it's highly unlikely. And if that happened, you'd think we would've heard him hollering or something."

Separate conversations broke out around the table. Willy and Tommy sat still, shaking their heads, shell-shocked. The Flintstones got up and headed for their dune buggy, saying they should join in the search before it got dark.

I checked the sky, the sun had just set. "You'll never get out there in time, and I'm sure the authorities are conducting a thorough search."

Wilma grabbed Fred by the arm, stopping him from climbing into his chariot. "We know the beach and back roads around there...but you're right, it will be too dark to see anything. We'll head out in the morning...it's the least we can do. Allison will be pulling her hair out."

The mayor commented on how our murder club wasn't accomplishing much, that if we weren't involving the police maybe we needed to pool our resources and hire a private detective, like Fred said. "What do you think, Ed?"

I thought about my response. "There's a lot of strange shit going on around here lately...more so since the arrival of our bottle guy, Amigo...anyone else notice that?"

GP asked what the hell I was talking about and did I suspect him of something?

"Think about it for a minute...the guy appears out of nowhere, naked on our beach. He can't speak and has no memory of who he is or where he's from. And he's got a strange mark on his neck just like Bruce, who didn't have it before he went missing and doesn't remember how."

GP scoffed. "You're really reaching, detective, you think the bottle guy is snatching people and what...sucking the flesh off their bones? And what do you mean he and Bruce have the same mark?"

Willy cut in. "Edmundo's right. I saw it too...same dots in a V shape on his neck. And Bruce has been spending a lot of time with

Amigo lately...he's even got him reading and writing now. Did you know that?"

"No, I didn't. And that's not what I said, GP. I'm simply gathering evidence and looking for connections...and from what Willy just said, there are lots more between Bruce and Amigo. I know you all think it's ridiculous, but Doreen told Katie and I that her cats have gone missing from time to time. She feels they've been abducted and it has something to do with strange lights she saw in the sky near Barra...by the golf course, actually."

GP laughed out loud. "C'mon, Ed, Katie's right...you've been watching too many alien shows."

I forced a laugh. "I know but I'm open to a better theory if anyone has one. Did you ever notice dogs or cats when Amigo is around?"

Laughter continued but Helen spoke up. "Ed's right. Coco loves everyone but won't go anywhere near that man. And neither will Janine's dog...she won't stop barking when Amigo is around."

Willy asked, "What are we gonna do about Gary?"

GP replied. "Don't worry, Ed's gonna have Amigo call the mother ship to have him returned. Gimme that bottle of tequila, Tommy."

CHAPTER NINETEEN

Getting Answers

My morning walks were far more than exercise. It was my time to think and reflect about what was happening in my life and where I wanted to be. Sometimes I'd form the next few chapters of the book I was working on, in my mind. Or or think about our next travel destination and plan the route in my head. We're more travelers than vacationers, with the exception of staying put for three months in Melaque. But we take side trips and Sunday drives.

Using my brain to consider clues, evidence, or murder suspects was not something I normally spent time doing. Even when I worked for a living, as a cop for over thirty years. I gave whatever case I was working on my full attention but I rarely took the job home with me. There is more to life than work and I did my best to live up to that philosophy.

But last night's missing person and the murder club's discussion consumed my thoughts as I weaved my way through Melaque's cobbled and broken streets. 'Look up, look down' was something you had to keep in mind to stay on your feet and not end up in a face plant on the pavement. Many found out the hard way, including

Big Willy who went down hard after having one too many on his birthday.

Victor waived at me, as he drove by on his ATV. Shit, I hadn't thought about him. He and his wife were Canadian expats who'd lived in Melaque for years and knew many of the locals. I made a mental note to hit him up on Facebook and pick his brain. Aliens came to mind again, maybe it was the strange-looking meth-head I saw coming out of the local drug den and into the morning light.

I couldn't say that anything extraterrestrial was responsible for what was happening in our little town, and it was obvious by the murder club's reaction that they thought I was crazy for even mentioning it. I've always been a believer we are not alone in the universe. I question whether other beings have visited or ever inhabited our blue planet.

A personal experience in Northern Ontario a few years earlier, strengthened my beliefs in UFO's after personally witnessing a strange object in the sky. I based my book, Four, on the unusual sighting.

Katie and I and two friends were sitting by a campfire, watching the sky for shooting stars, when we noticed one in particular. It looked like any other star but this one moved much slower than any falling or shooting stars I'd ever seen. It stopped and changed directions. We all saw it. Two more changes in direction and the strange object zipped off the way it came. In awe, we discussed what the object wasn't because of its trajectory and changes in direction. The space station, shooting stars, and Chinese lanterns were all ruled out. It was an unidentifiable flying object.

That didn't mean Melaque had been invaded and they were abducting people and animals. Did it? It was highly unlikely and I knew better. During my career in policing, I'd witnessed people do all kinds of unthinkable and unbelievable things to each other. I truly believe anyone's capable of murder or harming another, if put in the right situation. It's human nature.

I noticed the barber shop was empty and wondered if I needed a haircut. Then I saw Dr. Lee on his balcony, overlooking the street. He waived. Unaware of whether or not it was his residence, I stopped and waived back. The doctor pointed to the doorway below. He was halfway down the stairs when I got to the open door. I politely refused his extended hand, pointing out my wet appendage and how profusely I was perspiring. Lee asked if I wanted to come in. He had information from me.

I was anxious to hear what he said had to say but declined with an apology about my sweaty condition. He laughed. "It's okay, I wanted you to know they identified the bones you saw at the lagoon as belonging to the retired teacher from Villa Obregon. He who went missing while walking his dog. They haven't identified the other bones yet."

I played dumb. "There were more?"

"Yes, a woman's arm. They are still searching the lagoon for more remains."

"Crocodiles with scalpels again?"

He smiled, excused himself, and retreated up the stairs to answer his phone.

CHAPTER TWENTY

Pyramids

As usual on our winter stays down south, Katie and I took a side trip. We decided to visit the ancient City of Teotihuacan, home of the Great Pyramids of the Sun and Moon. It's only an hour from Mexico City. We flew into the capitol city and took a bus to the town of San Juan, just outside the Mayan ruin site. Staying three nights allowed us two full days to explore the complex.

An afternoon arrival gave us time to check out our neighborhood and the local market in downtown San Juan. It was like a giant tent city, wrapped around a building packed with stalls selling everything from vegetables to tequila and tacos. We sampled some Mexican street food while we browsed and dodged the hordes of shoppers.

After respecting Mexican customs and having a late afternoon siesta, we returned to the market area for dinner. We found a mom-and-pop restaurant, where they seated us at a table on a balcony overlooking the busy main street. Perfect for people watching and viewing the sunset behind a church steeple. A puffy cloud was perched behind the cross, with a beam of sunlight radiating all around it. Some might have called it a heavenly sight.

I felt a bit off the next morning, as we headed to the ruin site to meet our pre-arranged tour guide. There are certain times and places where using a knowledgeable professional is the way to go if you want the full cultural experience. There's nothing worse than paying to look at ruins when you don't have a clue about what you're seeing.

After meeting our guide at the gate, he recommended we buy hats to protect us from the sun, which was already hot enough at nine in the morning to melt candle wax. I had read it was a good idea and not just our man's attempt to have us buy something from one of his cousins. Within twenty minutes and no shade in sight, I knew it was a great five-dollar investment.

About an hour into the tour, I felt worse. Not sure if it was the heat or something I ate, or both, I told the guide to carry on with Katie for a bit and check back with me in twenty minutes or so. He thought about it and agreed I didn't look so well. I knew his fee was non-refundable but didn't care at that point since passing out or throwing up seemed imminent.

The guide walked us back to the gate and insisted he drive us back to our hotel where I could rest up. That I did, sleeping right through the rest of that day and night. By the next morning I was ready to take on the world again. Our park passes were good for another day so we visited the temple site on our own, using what we learned the previous day to get around.

Built over 1,500 years ago, Teotihuacan was the largest city in the Americas at the time, with a population of over 125,000 inhabitants, making it the sixth largest city in the world. We headed to the giant Pyramid of the Sun first. Katie climbed to the top for an overall view of the entire site. She looked about the size of an ant when she reached the 215-foot summit.

A wide paved road, about a kilometer long called Avenue of the Dead, links the Sun and Moon temples, along with many smaller religious sites. Some of them were adorned with ancient murals of Mayan or Aztec warriors and Jaguars. As with the pyramids in Egypt and other magnificent ruin sites around the world, today's expert engineers and builders are still at a loss to explain the ancient construction methods.

We had a great day exploring and found a really cool restaurant for dinner. The whole dining experience took place underground in a limestone cave. The large opening allows in fresh air and natural light, until dusk when lanterns on the natural rock walls come to life. National dishes and desserts were tasty and top notch, making for a truly unique cultural experience.

Later, back in the hotel room, I sorted my photographs and checked email. There was a message from the mayor at our resort in Melaque. Amigo had been arrested.

CHAPTER TWENTY-ONE

Home Invasion

All the other people in Melaque lived indoors, inside buildings or structures that contained various furnishings, depending on their status. Amigo didn't mind his little hidden retreat. It hadn't rained since he moved in and he'd even managed to accumulate some of his own furniture. He found it amazing what other people discarded without a second thought. An air mattress, table, chair, and a pan for cooking. What more could he want?

There was no need for a clock, he simply got up when the sun illuminated his colored glass wall and went to bed when it got dark. On this particular morning, he read a book his friend Bruce gave him; a story about other people and their troubles in a place called Ireland. Amigo discovered he could read and understand both English and Spanish, but not the language the people from Quebec spoke.

Hearing a rustling sound outside his shack, Amigo pulled the curtain back to have a look. A black metal pipe was placed between his eyes. A gun. From their fixed position on the weapon, his eyes moved to the man in front of him. Dressed in a military uniform, the soldier spoke in Spanish, demanding he put his hands above his head and come outside.

Amigo complied and saw there were more soldiers circling his home with all their weapons pointed directly at him. The man who told him to come out asked his name and for proof of identity. Amigo grunted, the only sound his vocal cords allowed, and offered his empty palms as a sign he had no proof of anything.

Another man wearing a bulky vest that said, Policia, grabbed and threw him face-first to the ground. His jaws still open trying to speak, Amigo got a mouthful of sand. Two of the soldiers ripped the sheet from his doorway and searched inside his hovel. They kicked and tossed his things around and one of them knocked over his wall of glass bottles, shattering many of them.

They spoke to each other in Spanish and one of the men who searched his place handed the policeman a wallet found inside the shack. He opened it and pulled out an Ontario Teachers Federation ID card in the name of Dale Gauthier. The officer held the card beside Amigo's face, comparing it to the image. They weren't even close.

The Mexican cop went ballistic, demanding to know where he got the wallet and if he knew the man in the photograph. Amigo did his best to speak but only made noises that aggravated his interrogator even more. Handcuffed and still on his knees in the sand, the officer kicked him in the stomach causing him to fall on his face again.

The soldiers who searched Amigo's shack tore it down and searched the debris again. Acting on orders, they picked him up from the ground and carried him off. What was left of Amigo's home crunched beneath the retreating boots of soldiers. His little house was nothing but scattered debris and pieces of colored glass sparkling in the morning light.

CHAPTER TWENTY-TWO

Robin

We got back to our resort after dinner and found the gang gathered under the pergola, drinking wine and eating a coconut cream pie Wilma made. They welcomed us home and Wanda asked about our trip. Katie filled them in. Assuming I was thirsty after our little getaway, GP handed me a beer. I don't know why I bothered to buy my own, he was very generous with his.

I raised my can to his glass of scotch and let my wife finish reciting our travelogue. Big Willy was sitting beside me and tapped my arm. He offered one of his scrunched-up pouty faces and nodded towards the Batman, who sat across the table. Bruce's head was down and he wore an expression more suited for a family wake.

"What's up with him?" I asked.

Willy mimicked Bruce's soured face. "He's upset about Dick getting busted."

I paused, eyed Bruce for a second and turned back to Willy. "I give...who's Dick?"

Willy made another face, as if his expression was my clue. "You know...Batman and Robin..."

It took a few seconds but it dawned on me. "Oh...Dick Grayson. Okay, again...who's Dick?"

"Amigo. He and Bruce have been spending more time together than the Dynamic Duo. The cops arrested him while you were gone. For murder."

Katie was listening in and we both spoke at the same time. "What?"

Helen took over. "They raided his shack by the lagoon and found stuff that belonged to the teacher...the bones we saw."

Fred offered more. "Wilma and I were coming down the beach in the buggy and saw soldiers and cops taking him away in cuffs."

GP scoffed. "Guess that puts an end to the murder club. I knew that guy was no good. Amigo...Dick...whoever he was."

Fred responded. "No, I didn't see his dick...he was wearing clothes this time."

Wilma shook her head and playfully wiped a bit of whipped cream from his moustache. "We waited until the cops were out of sight and checked out what was left of his shack. It was completely destroyed. And there were all sorts of bones in the fire pit...not human...small animals like dogs and cats, maybe."

Sticks groaned and held her stomach, as if she was about to heave. "Dogs and cats, what the heck?"

"It's no wonder Coco and other canines didn't like him." Helen added.

Bruce snapped out of his drunken stupor. "They got the wrong guy...Amigo wouldn't hurt anyone. He's a victim just like me."

"Victim?" I asked. "How's that, Bruce?"

His speech was slurred. "He disappeared like me and don't remember nothing about it. Maybe we were abducted like Donna's cats."

"You mean Doreen?"

"Her too? See, Ed, maybe you're right about aliens...you catch the congressional hearings in the states? Whistle blowers telling us how the government's been lying to us since Roswell...they have flying saucers and little grey men on ice somewhere."

It was the first I'd heard about the hearings but would surely look it up. No surprise to me...our governments had been covering shit up for years. It was about time someone spoke up. I could only imagine the effect on the world if the whole truth got out and the panic it might cause. We'd been lied to for so long, many people wouldn't know the truth even when they heard it.

I expected GP to laugh but he looked serious when he spoke. "I don't know anything about UFO's and aliens but I witnessed my share of government cover-ups when I was in the military. There were always rumors about guys who saw weird shit they couldn't explain but we just laughed at them, figuring they were smoking weed to pass the time."

Bruce did his best to stay focused and involved in the conversation. "There's no way Amigo killed anyone." He pulled down his shirt collar. "We have the same re-birth marks...like brothers from different mothers. Murder club or whatever...we need to find the truth."

Big Willy slammed his fist on the table. "This sounds like a job for Mulder and Scully."

CHAPTER TWENTY-THREE

All Quiet on the Beachfront

The next week was uneventful. Maybe it was only a few days, who knows? They say time flies, but when you're retired your life boards a jet and takes you to the future, where your body ages faster than your brain. Or so it seems when every day has become a holiday. I know we're all dying a little bit each day, but do my knees, hips and back have to remind me of it all the time?

I'm not one to complain about life. Katie and I remind each other all the time how lucky we are to have what we do. Raised by a single mother who worked three jobs to keep her six children fed and clothed, I learned to appreciate the value of a dollar and what it took to earn it. Retirement is the best job I've ever had, but it was no piece of cake getting here.

There were some bumps and personal losses along the way, but I am happy with my life. And my second wife, who I discovered on a dating site called Plenty of Fish. Katie, is the best thing I ever caught. We have a great thing together. But she still laughs at me when I rant about bent politicians or the possibility of extraterrestrial life forms.

Did I really think Amigo and Bruce and Doreen's cats were ab-ducted by aliens? Having been a cop for thirty-one years and seeing what the human race was capable of on its own, I have to say no. But it doesn't mean my mind's not open to the possibility there are phenomenon I can't explain. I think being open-minded is one trait that helped me become a good detective.

I had no idea who might be responsible for the missing and murdered in Melaque. How could I be, with only hearsay, rumor and innuendo to go on? I did wonder what evidence authorities had on Amigo. Surely, him being in possession of someone else's wallet wasn't enough to hold him for murder.

I knew they did things different in Mexico, but I also had to wonder what led the cops to Amigo in the first place. Were they under pressure to satisfy the concerns of worried tourists who are their bread and butter along the Costalegre? Perhaps Amigo, a transient nobody, was the perfect patsy. Did they have real evidence against him? Nobody really knew the man, where he came from, or what kind of past life he had.

Peace and quiet meant more time on the keyboard for me, where I could decide who would live and who would die in Abigail Brown's fictional world. Some fans hinted they hoped Norm and Abigail got back together. Women. They are my biggest fans but and are always looking for romance, even in crime novels. It can be challenging writing sex scenes, and even a little embarrassing at times when my wife reads it.

I did a podcast interview where the host asked me if Abigail was a real person. Even one of my sisters said she didn't remember me dating a black police woman from Detroit. I laughed. Like most of my characters, she was pieced together using quirks and traits of other women I worked with over the years. That's where writing fiction can be fun.

But we live in a non-fictional world and it tells me there is more human carnage in our future and the arrest of Amigo won't be the end of it.

CHAPTER TWENTY-FOUR

80

Another day...another party. This time it was Morty's eightieth birthday bash, held at the same place as all the other birthday parties. Julio's. Knowing the bar would be packed and food service slow, Katie and I ate at home before catching up with some of the gang and buying Morty his birthday shot. Same as me, he was a retired police detective, but he did his bit in Los Angles. We always said we should swap stories someday but it never happened. Who better to get details about juicy murder investigations from than a real-life big city homicide detective?

Morty was now an expat, having moved to Melaque after tiring of life in LA and its associated cost of living. He admitted it was a challenge living full-time in Mexico but his cop pension allowed him to live like a king.

The last two seats in the bar were at Willy and Wanda's table so we joined them. Already perspiring from the ten-minute walk over, I switched on the nearby floor fan and pointed it directly at Big Willy and me. He gave me the thumbs up. The waitress appeared at our table and paused in front of the fan. She was soaked in sweat, far worse off than me. Katie and I ordered a couple beers and a shot of whatever Morty was drinking.

Her return took a while, no surprise to us. Wanda said they'd ordered food over an hour earlier and wondered if they'd ever get it. Willy wore one of his pouty faces and told us they were so busy that Julio had the place next door bringing in food from their kitchen. It looked like there was a break in the action around Morty's table so I walked over with his birthday shot. He laughed when I added it to the waiting line of shot glasses in front of him.

"Happy birthday young man! Looks like you've got your work cut out for you."

"Thanks, Ed. It's gonna be a long night. Can't put 'em back like I used to."

"I hear ya, brother, I'm a lightweight now compared to what I drank back in the day."

He picked up my gift. "Where's yours?"

"Sorry, never been partial to pounding shots, no offence."

He threw back the glass of tequila. "By the way...I liked your book. Tommy gave it to me earlier as a birthday present. It's very well-written."

"Thanks, man that means a lot coming from an old gumshoe like you. We really do have to get together and talk shop. Maybe I can write one of your stories."

Morty did another shot. Judging by the empties on the table, it surprised me he was still able to carry on a conversation. But he was a big man, taller and wider than me, with a larger holding tank. Another couple came up to his table with birthday wishes so I stepped back.

"We'll make a point of getting together, Ed, thanks for the shot."

Half-way back to our table I remembered that I wanted to ask Morty if he heard or knew anything about the missing and murdered in town. Being a permanent resident, I assumed he had connections and was privy to more information than me and the murder club. Maybe we should have invited him to be a member. Willy and Wanda's food was on the table when I got back. I stole a couple of Willy's fries when he wasn't looking.

CHAPTER TWENTY-FIVE

Two Moons

Morty's birthday party wound down early, as with most of our shindigs in Melaque. As retired seniors, we got at it early so we could be in bed by nine. That wasn't the case on this evening because Katie caught wind of a lunar eclipse taking place after dark. Though the street lights were on, when mom would have expected me home, I agreed to hang out and maybe even howl at the moon.

Big Willy, Wanda, Katie and I worked our way down the beach to join the rest of our clan at the resort table. In truth, the women walked the beach but Willy and I took the street to avoid getting sand between our toes. GP and Bruce waived us in on approach, pointing to the empty seats they saved. Helen and Sticks were only steps away, glasses and bottles of wine in hand.

A swath of burnt orange and blood red stretched from the southern skyline and disappeared behind the mountain at the west end of the beach. The ocean was resting for the night, its surface reflecting the colorful sunset. Katie asked what time the eclipse would be so GP put his thumb up to the moon and predicted what time it would be.

Bruce laughed. "Don't you usually tell time by the sun?"

GP scoffed. "It's 8:35pm right now."

Bruce rolled his eyes. "I call bullshit."

Sticks checked her phone. "He's right, Bruce, I have 8:36."

Defeated, he cracked another beer. By the looks of him, he'd been that way since dinner time. He and Sticks had gone off on their own, to their favorite Chinese food restaurant. GP tapped my leg and tilted his head down. My eyes followed his direction and I saw he had Helen's phone in his hand. It showed the current time on the display. "Cheater...here I thought it was some trick you picked up in the army."

I felt a presence behind me just before the back of my chair sunk into the sand. Morty was standing there, leaning on it for support. I was surprised and impressed at the same time. He was still able to stand.

"Hey, Ed, I didn't get a chance to chat much at my party but wanted to talk about the homicides in town." He swayed a bit and had a thick tongue but he was quite coherent. "Is this your murder club?"

GP was within earshot. "That's what we call it but we haven't figured out shit...except for Bruce over there, who's all broken up about his brother getting arrested for murdering the teacher and dumping him in the lagoon."

Morty attempted to lean closer to GP but he lost his balance for a second. He wasn't as steady on his feet as I thought. His wife grabbed ahold of his arm in an attempt to steady him. "C'mon, detective, we need to get you home." Being about half his size, she never could have stopped him from going down.

He turned to look at me and wet his lips with his tongue as if thinking and preparing to say something. "I...no, you are right baby, I think we need to get home." He was already spun around when he said, "We'll talk more later Ed, there's weird shit going on around here." Morty did a big wave across the air, signaling his fare-well to all.

We had Pink Floyd's Dark Side of the Moon and some ERA playing for effect while we watched the moon rise above the ocean in its attempt to reach the stars. The resort manager agreed to shut all the non-essential outdoor lights off so we could get the full Milky Way effect. We watched for the International Space Station, shooting stars, and whatever other extraterrestrial phenomenon we might be lucky enough to see.

One of our neighbors entertained us by reporting which destinations particular aircraft were heading to as they crossed the sky above. A first for most of us, we learned he had an app on his phone that supplied him with that information. I wondered how it would work for UFO's. Having that thought, I glanced over at Bruce. He hadn't been the same since Amigo was arrested.

Faint Oohs and ahs fell from parted lips as planet earth cast a shadow on its moon. I'd seen solar and lunar eclipses before. The latter wasn't as impressive to watch but I thought it was pretty cool when considering how everything was in motion. The moon, earth, sun, and our whole ever-expanding universe.

Not to be outdone by an astronomical event, GP called out to our table. He'd positioned himself between us and the ocean, with his pants down around his ankles. "Look, everyone...there's two full moons!"

We laughed and carried on, getting kind of bored with the whole eclipse thing. It wasn't only the full moon that was glowing, Katie suggested we all go streaking down the beach. There were no takers and it was then we noticed Bruce was gone. Sticks said she thought he was getting more beer. Someone else said he went for a pee.

The more we talked about it and considered Bruce's history, Sticks voiced her concern. We agreed he wasn't himself and maybe we needed to find him. Katie said it was such a beautiful night, she wanted to walk the beach. She and Wanda said they'd head east and keep an eye out for him. Sticks went with them and Helen talked GP into checking west. He grumbled but went along. Willy and I said we'd check the bar and any stores nearby that sold beer.

Unbeknownst to the rest of us, the women found Bruce a short time later down by Twiggs bar. He was soaking wet and right out of it. Katie told me later he was in some sort of trance; on his knees in the sand and staring off into the night sky beyond Isla de Navidad. He was almost incoherent and kept mumbling something about lights in the sky.

CHAPTER TWENTY-SIX

Who You Know

There were a couple of party-less days to recuperate after the double feature of birthday party and lunar eclipse. I hadn't seen Bruce since the night he wandered off again, but Katie was in a group text with the girls where Sticks said he still wasn't himself. The only explanation he offered her was that he was drawn to the lights behind the mountain on Isla de Navidad and almost drowned trying to swim there. Once again, his memory was foggy, probably booze related.

We'd heard didley-squat about poor Gary. A search of the area came up negative, with the exception of his shoe and club they found. What happened to him? Did he accidentally play someone else's ball, an egotistical or homicidal cartel dude? It didn't seem likely. As usual, local authorities had no answers and told his family to wait it out and he would turn up eventually. Right, maybe with his bones stripped of their flesh and found in the lagoon.

It was a breakfast-out day for me, something I did at least once a week during my morning walks. Being a bacon and egg kind of guy, I'd seek out places that catered to gringos for exactly that. I'm not into the yellow, green or brown colored Mexican slop that looks like something scooped from a baby's diaper. Give me fat from a pig's ass and eggs from a chicken's bum-hole any day.

I stopped at one of my go-to places along the beach on the return half of my stroll. A quiet and shady spot to watch local fishermen bringing in the morning catch, and a few crazy old people who swam laps in the ocean every morning. One actually had a heart attack right after his morning swim one day. Go figure, they say exercise is supposed to be good for you.

Before I could grab my usual seat, Morty called out to me. He said he just ordered, if I wanted to join him. I already knew exactly what I wanted so I informed the waiter on the way to the table. Morty looked a little rough in the morning light. I wondered if it was the effects of a two-day hangover or I simply hadn't noticed before. Old pock marks and heavy creases on his forehead, helped to give away his age.

Somehow, he seemed tired too. Not of life itself, but perhaps the years of public service in one of the busiest and baddest cities in the U.S. We got the cordial stuff about the weather and shitty Mexican food we both hated for breakfast out of the way. After the waiter dropped off his coffee and my ice water and diet coke, Morty said, "What the hell is going on in our little piece of paradise?"

I shook my head. "I don't know, Amigo, in short I think we've either got a serial killer on the loose or aliens are abducting people and animals to conduct experiments."

He blew through puckered lips to cool his coffee and took a sip. "I see you've been talking to Doreen about her cats."

I shrugged. "Yeah, I thought it was only the wine talking, but she seriously believes someone's messing with her animals. I took it with a grain of salt, having one of my own cats disappear for two months in winter, only to come home in the spring." I chuckled. "Come to think of it though, he had a strange injury that could have been from an alien experiment."

Stifling a laugh, Morty unintentionally dipped his top lip into the cup. "Shit...that's hot. You're not a coffee drinker, Ed?"

I had polished off half my ice water. "Negative, I don't like any hot beverages...with maybe the exception of a hot chocolate once or twice in cold weather. I sweat enough on the outside; I can't imagine putting something hot inside me. What do you think is going on around here?"

Morty glanced back toward the kitchen. "They surely take their time cooking our meals...must've gone to the chicken coop for fresh eggs. You called me Amigo earlier. I know for sure that guy was nabbed by the Mexican authorities to save face, in an attempt to silence us tourists."

I checked the kitchen too, there didn't seem to be much action back there. "Save face, really? Have you heard something from someone other than the local grapevine?"

Morty eyed his half-empty cup for a second, then held it up and tried to catch the waiter's attention. His eyes shifted to the sound of squawking in the surf where a group of seagulls' dive bombed what was probably a school of baitfish. "You know how it works Ed, it's always who you know and what they know."

Having finished my ice water, I started on my pop. "So, you've got a guy...anything you've heard that you'd like to share?"

"Chief of Police in Cihuatlan...met him years ago in LA when he was in town for an international Chiefs convention."

I pushed myself back in my chair. "Wow, the big kahuna, can't get any better than that."

"Yeah, but you know even bosses have bosses and it ain't no different here in Mexico. Anyway, they assigned me as his driver...Senior Alvarez. He requested someone from Hollywood Homicide because he thought we were all famous...wanted me to introduce him to Bullitt and Dirty Harry. I had to explain that they were fictional characters in San Francisco."

I laughed. "So, he's a little geographically challenged?"

"That's putting it politely. Seriously, I don't know how the man ever became chief. But he loves fishing and invited me down here for a charter on his brother-in-law's boat. That's how I was introduced to Melaque."

Still sweating from my brisk walk and the morning sun reflecting off the beach, I dabbed my forehead with a napkin. "Cool. Do you still go fishing with him?"

"Hell yeah. It's free with him...I can't afford the prices they charge for those charters on my cop pension. We were out just last week, after they arrested Amigo for the murder of the retired teacher. I waited until he had a few beers into him before I brought it up—the man can drink tequila like water but he's buzzed after three beers.

I asked Alvarez what he could tell me about Amigo. He said finding the victim's wallet in his shack was enough to hold him and he'd have to appear in court at a later date."

My stomach growled so loud Morty stopped talking for a moment. We both turned to see what was happening in the kitchen. The waiter was chatting with the cook and was oblivious to the two really big men who were about to storm the kitchen. "You must have wondered what sent the cops to Amigo in the first place...nobody really knows him...shit, he doesn't even know himself."

"Yeah, I asked but he never answered the question. But later in the conversation, after another beer, he mentioned something about a French guy who got into it with Amigo on the beach after he picked up their empty bottles. He droned on and on about how they have to keep the tourists happy in these small towns and his orders came from higher up."

"Like you said, right? Someone tipped off the right politician...isn't that how things really get done in Mexico?"

The waiter appeared, put our food on the table, and took a step back—probably afraid that one of us would nick him with a fork or knife in our feeding frenzy. We asked for salt and ketchup and put our conversation on hold while we dug in. Silence fell over our table, making the waves and seagulls and other patrons around us seem louder. Filling our bellies, not solving crime, was our common goal.

My wife says I'm a fast eater, something I learned to do early in life when competing with five siblings for food, but Morty's technique brought him the championship. Shoving whole pieces of bacon in my mouth to save chewing time, I watched the retired murder cop's means of attack, hoping to pick up some tips on speed. It was all in his posture, he leaned over his plate putting less distance between his mouth and food. Like the shovel on a backhoe, his arm and fork worked in sync.

Graciously accepting defeat, I relaxed in my chair and ran the last few home fries through ketchup before popping them into my mouth. Morty used his third coffee to wash down any lingering remains of his breakfast. He picked up exactly where he left off in the conversation, which seemed like it ended only seconds ago.

"Maybe a silly question, Ed, but do you know any politicians in this country? That's the approach if we want to get the police off their asses."

"As a matter of fact, I do. Doctor Lee...you must know him?"

"The guy who owns the bar down the street and has bikes and cars driving all over town, blaring advertisements over loudspeakers? Everyone in town knows him but I thought it was because of his former medical practice and the restaurant/bar he runs now."

I pushed my empty plate aside and swallowed the last of my diet coke. "The man's worn many hats...doctor, musician, land and bar owner, and politician. He's held many offices locally and at the state level. Lee stood beside the Governor at the ribbon cutting of the new malecon a couple weeks ago. He's the one who pushed the state to replace the bridge there"

Morty nodded along, looking impressed. He wiped his mouth with a napkin, just in case any of his breakfast missed its target. "Huh, I didn't know he was connected politically."

"Still is...and he knows the local ME...told me how the flesh appeared to have been surgically removed from the bones and where unusual scrape marks were found."

"What? That's a new one on me...and I've seen all sorts of weird shit. I assumed crocodiles feasted on him."

"So did everyone else. Even the ME was stymied, thinking maybe the brittle bones were boiled in something like bleach. They haven't identified the woman's remains yet and I hear they're still searching the lagoon to make sure there aren't any other victims in there."

Morty's eyes never left mine. He remained silent for a moment, absorbing what he just heard. I could almost hear his wheels turning, once a detective—always a detective. "Fuck me, Ed, that's some pretty wild shit we've got going on around here. Is the doc part of your murder club?"

"You know about that, huh? I don't play bridge and they say to go with what you know." I smiled. "Why, you want in for fun...relive the old days?"

He chuckled. "Fred told me about it. I'm busy enough doing nothing every day and having all the time in the world to do it. Melaque is my home now though, and my cop senses are screaming at me to get some answers as to what's going on."

The waiter picked up our discarded dishes and dropped off our receipts. Morty grabbed mine before I could. "When's your next club meeting?"

CHAPTER TWENTY-SEVEN

Jorge

With the exception of Bruce, all members of the murder club were in attendance at our resort. At my invitation, Morty joined us for the fun of it. He wore a big smile. "Where else can you go for happy hour and talk about missing and murdered people. You folks make an old cop shy."

The sheriff called the meeting to order and appointed GP as Sergeant at Arms. He graciously accepted the position on the condition the new guy did a welcome shot of tequila. Morty smiled and complied. "I like this club...kinda reminds me of the old days when we debriefed at the local pub after solving a case. Guess we got some work to do here before that happens."

On my go-ahead the new guy filled in the group about his buddy, the police chief, and what he knew and didn't know. The group listened intently, the only sound being Big Willy crunching potato chips. He stopped mid-chew when he realized how loud it was, and tried to swallow what was in his mouth. I thought he'd choke, but he managed to wash it down with beer.

I updated the group on my latest intel from Doctor Lee, mentioning his medical and political connections and how Morty and I thought we'd found the key to busting our investigation wide open. Everyone in town knew the doc, and Helen agreed he was a good man to get things done.

Fred leaned in over the table, straining to hear,. I should have seen it coming. "Ed saw the doctor again...what's the matter with his dick now?"

We all laughed. Poor Fred, he was too easy to pick on, but thankfully he had a great sense of humor. GP told Morty how he teased Fred every once-in-a-while by shouting, "Timber!" His natural reflex always caused him to duck or flinch. It was a mean prank and not really funny, but we laughed anyway. Humor was one of the attributes that made life fun for all of us at the resort, and why we all got along so well.

Morty reached across the table for peanuts. "You're an asshole, GP...my kinda guy."

Seeing that everyone's attention was on him, Fred updated us on information he and Wilma were able to solicit from some of the locals they knew. Out of our group at the resort, the Flintstones had been coming to Melaque the longest. Of everyone else we knew, only Morty had been coming longer.

Wilma said there were some Americans who reported their daughter missing, after spending a couple weeks in Barra de Navidad. The young girl met a local guy and decided to stay on after her parents flew back home. They reached out to authorities when they couldn't contact her. After a cold reception from police, they contacted American media. According to her parents, their daughter told them her lover ran a limousine company. They later found out he was a simple taxi driver named Jorge and he lived in the barrio, east of town.

Morty interjected. "Jorge? That's not good. Folks around here have been complaining about him forever. He tried to rip Margie and I off once, after driving us back from La Manzanilla. He's offensive and especially aggressive towards women. I've heard rumors of sexual assault and rape...and get this...his cab number is 69."

Sticks asked, "Do the police know that...have they done anything about it?"

Morty shrugged. GP replied for him. "It's Mexico."

The retired LA detective continued. "The cops know about him...or at least my police chief buddy does. He told me once Jorge is untouchable."

"What does that mean?" Katie asked.

"He's probably connected to the cartel in some way...using that clout to get away with whatever he wants."

There was grumbling around the table. Helen said, "That's just wrong in so many ways. I thought the cartel didn't want anyone messing with tourists...we are part of their livelihood."

I cut in. "I'm sure there are exceptions to every rule. Maybe he's some cartel dude's spoiled brat who's out of control and does things just to piss off daddy. Can you reach out to your guy, Morty, and see if the cops think the female bones recovered in the lagoon belong to the American woman?"

"Sure, we're due for a fishing trip. You wanna come, Ed?"

"I'm not much into deep sea fishing but won't turn down the chance to question a police chief as to why they're not all over this Jorge guy, connected or not."

"He'd certainly be at the top of my suspect list if I was part of these investigations. I'll set it up."

GP busied himself setting up a round of shots, in case the meeting was over. "Hey, anyone know what the hell is going on with Bruce?"

CHAPTER TWENTY-EIGHT

Swamped

For me, morning is the best time to see the beach. An arch of red and orange and yellow pushed its way into blue, reflecting off the ocean's surface as the tide ferried waves ashore. Nature seemed at peace in the morning, before humans disturbed the serenity. But something unusual caught my eye during my walk along the beach road.

Large flotillas of plants were dragged along the riptide, some littering the beach like piles of seaweed deposited after a storm. I recognized the water hyacinths that grew abundantly in the lagoon and realized what was happening. Normally, it was only during the rainy season when locals broke open the natural sand berm that separated the lagoon from the ocean. They did it to prevent flooding in town but I'd never seen it done during tourist season.

Being the curious sort, I continued walking east to check things out. When I neared the lagoon, I saw men standing on both sides of the river they'd created. Flora and Fauna alike flowed out to sea, resembling a row of floats in the Rose Bowl parade. Whatever was in the lagoon was now drifting along the shoreline, not a pretty sight for tourists and beach lovers.

One of the men screamed at a small crocodile that managed to swim back to the beach, preferring its warm freshwater home to the new cooler saltwater surroundings. I shook my head, wondering how many more of those things would surprise sunbathers and swimmers on the beach that day.

Coming up on the man furthest away from the crocodile, I used my best Spanglish to ask him what was going on. He pointed further inland, where I saw men in small boats paddling around the lagoon. Were they still searching for bodies or bones? I wondered. Needing answers personally and for our murder club, I walked up the malecon.

There were more men along the lagoon's shoreline and some in waders, poking around in the weeds and muck with wooden poles. The water level was the lowest I'd ever seen it, the muddy bottom visible in many areas. Two men shouting caught my attention, and by the level of excitement in their voices I assumed it was another crocodile.

One of them reached down into the murky water and came up with an arm. They'd found another body. The other searchers moved toward them as the second guy pulled up a leg. My heart skipped a beat. It was morbid but cool at the same time, I couldn't wait to report back to the murder club. Then the two men held the body up over their heads as if they'd just won the Stanley Cup. It had no head.

It wasn't until laughter broke out amongst the searchers and I'd moved closer, that I realized they had found a manikin. The men in uniform barely moved and didn't seem amused. I assumed they'd seen their share of real bodies. I smiled at their discovery and had to admit it was kind of funny—probably a prank by one of the locals.

Taking in the activity in and around the lagoon, I surmised someone decided it was the easiest way to check for more human remains. Maybe the authorities were finally taking the situation seriously to appease all the snowbirds in town during their peak tourist season. Too bad they didn't consider all the shit from the lagoon now polluted the bay and washed up on the beach.

CHAPTER TWENTY-NINE

Wildfire

After my walk, I completed my morning ritual at the resort with a dip in the pool. This time it was the maid and her granddaughter who were entertained by the crazy Canadian taking his polar bear plunge. The locals didn't seem to have a problem with the water temperature at the beach and kids never have a problem with cold water in their pools.

I filled Katie in about the Mexican body retrieval efforts while I made my breakfast. She said it didn't surprise her. The American news stations were all over the story about the young white girl missing from a Mexican beach town. As far as we knew, the female remains in the lagoon hadn't been identified yet. If they belonged to an American, they might just invade the country.

I made a mental note to track down Doctor Lee and see if he knew any more about the remains. Maybe it was pressure from the north that had locals draining the lagoon. The news had already spread like a forest fire in high wind and we had friends on Facebook checking in to see if we were safe. They were killing cops back home but that wasn't newsworthy anymore.

Katie stuck her head out the patio door and told me she, Helen and GP were taking their bikes down to the lagoon to see what was going on. She commented earlier there was no use going to the beach because of the plants decaying in the hot sun, and the possibility of wayward crocodiles. They were barely out the gate when Fred and Wilma came downstairs. She popped her head around the corner of our patio and asked if I heard about them finding another body in the lagoon.

Considering whether or not I should tell them about the manikin, I scoffed and said I'd heard. They were on the way to check out the action too so why spoil their fun. I told them to let me know what else they found out.

Fred was already in the buggy calling for Wilma to move along. He squeaked a rubber chicken that hung from his rearview mirror. I bought it for his birthday. Wilma said he loved driving around town choking his chicken to make it chirp. The murder club hit the road. Katie texted Wanda, but she said Big Willy was hung over from our previous meeting, and he went to Julio's for his onion ring breakfast.

The resort seemed empty. I enjoyed the peace and quiet, a perfect time to write and get back into Abigail's murder story. It was time to give readers another clue about the killer. Maybe a tease about the real antagonist or perhaps a decoy to keep them guessing. I couldn't make it too easy to figure out, that's why crime fans love mysteries so much—anticipation and suspense—kind of like our murder club.

Some of us wondered about the man we called Amigo. Was he the killer? Or was it the new suspect, Jorge, the bad-boy cartel-connected cab driver who was said to be untouchable? I laughed inside. It would be hilarious and freaky at the same time if aliens were the real culprits. Body snatchers from another planet. The fiction elements grew heavy in my twisted mind.

I wondered what became of Amigo and if authorities would simply let him rot in an overpopulated prison somewhere. It made me think of Bruce. He was supposed to be proof-reading one of my crime stories but I hadn't heard anything from him since the eclipse party.

CHAPTER THIRTY

The Bean

Having slept in a bit, Katie asked if I was still planning on selling books at El Frijol that day. I completely forgot it was market day...something that happened to old retired people more often than not. I sat up in bed, scratched my head. "What time is it?"

"8:30. Wanda and I were going to take a taxi...it's too far for her to walk with her bad back. Can you give us a ride and pick us up when you're done at the coffee shop? I think Willy wants to come along and hang out with you."

I was on the toilet before she finished her sentence. "Thirty minutes? No problem as long as I get to poop first...you never know what the toilet there will be like."

"Yeah...I'm sure the customers there will appreciate that...why don't you use the toilet by the pool. You stink."

"And your shit smells like roses?"

"I don't shit...just drop marbles and they're odorless."

"What about your rotten egg farts?"

Katie ignored me and got her shopping bags ready. I brushed my teeth, popped my contacts in, and used a big glass of water to wash down my daily pills. Admiring myself in the mirror, I commented to my wife, "I can't wait until tomorrow…"

"Why's that, baby?"

"Cuz I get better looking every day." She fell for it every time.

I grabbed a leftover sausage and a cheese stick from the fridge, scooped up my box of books and headed to the door. "See…I'm ready and waiting for you. Again."

The plan was to try and sell my remaining copies of Trafficking Chen and Finding Hope that I had brought to Mexico. El Frijol was a coffee shop near the market where lots of gringos got their morning fix. I had pre-arranged the sale with the owner a couple weeks prior and hoped to take advantage of the people coming and going from the market.

We picked up Willy and Wanda Wonka in the Impala and headed to Villa Obregon, where the coffee shop and market were located. The big guy said he wanted to make one lap around the market and circle back to me. I found the last empty table and set out my books. Getting the stink-eye from a waiter, I ordered a blueberry muffin and diet coke.

Katie had told me how busy the coffee shop was, but I was blown away by the traffic. They could give Tim Hortons a run for their money. A woman I knew stopped to say hey and said she'd come back to buy my latest novel after she secured a table for her and some friends. Others glanced at my offerings but didn't line up for me like they did for their cup of joe.

About an hour later, I recognized the owner carrying in a box of coffee filters. He smiled and nodded and continued on to the kitchen. A short time later, he returned with a coffee in hand and took the empty seat across from me. I offered my hand and we shook, not sure he'd remember me or our agreement.

"I see you drink your own product."

He smiled, raised his glass cup and glanced at my coke. "Yes, we all have our ways to inject caffeine for a morning wakeup."

Rico spoke perfect English, maybe better than mine. He dressed well and smelled good, signs of a successful business man who also took care of himself. He had no Spanish or Mexican accent. I complimented him on his speech and asked where he learned it. Rico said he went to business school in San Diego and lived there for several years, before returning home. He thanked his parents for giving him that opportunity.

As busy as his place was, I thought he would leave me and get back to work. But he grabbed a copy of the Finding Hope and read the back cover. "Interesting...were you in law enforcement?"

"Yes, in Windsor, Ontario. A city cop for thirty-one years, I retired a detective and took up writing as a hobby. Do you read much?" It was a sales pitch; you always have to be selling.

"Yes...but not books per say. More business stuff...newspapers, periodicals to stay in touch." He scanned the crowd in his shop. "I really don't have the time. But this story of missing women intrigues me. Maybe you should write about the ones here in Melaque."

I was taken aback. "Do you know something about the missing and murdered we've been hearing about?"

Rico took a sip of coffee; his eyes were the same color as the dark roast in his cup. He grinned. "A serial killer, I think. My theory, based on the patterns."

A Frenchman picked up one of my books but my full attention was on the coffee shop owner."

"What patterns?"

My potential customer put the book down and walked away. A window shopper.

"He's selecting tourists, and always kills on market days."

His statement hit me in the face like hot coffee. "What? Do you have some special knowledge of the victims and when they've gone missing or have been killed?"

"They've all been customers...even the young American from Barra. I don't forget a face. The majority of them are regulars...like at your Tim Hortons. People have habits and like the same coffee every morning. And as you can see, market days are very busy around here. A perfect time to lose...or pick someone out of a crowd. And in each case, the last time I saw the victims was on market day."

I was blown away. "That's quite a theory. Have you spoken to the authorities about it?"

Rico chuckled. "Mexican authorities? That's a laugh. And it's only my theory."

Someone in the kitchen called out to him. He placed my book back on the pile and excused himself.

"So, that's your theory and you're sticking to it?"

Rico turned his head back to me as he walked away. "Unless you believe in alien abductions?"

Serial?

I couldn't wait to fill in the rest of the group. Trying to solve the Melaque murders had become a retirement pastime for our little group. Not that I believed we'd actually solve any of the killings or find any of the missing. It was kind of fun, in a twisted sort of way. For me, it was about re-igniting the flame inside me that burned out the day I retired. As far as the others, I think they enjoyed playing detective.

Books sales were slow so I was glad when Big Willy showed up. His forehead was covered in thick beads of sweat. He asked if they sold beer. I chuckled but knew where he was coming from. The sun had shifted and was invading my shady table. I checked the time. I was thinking about shutting it down, and asked Willy where the women were.

He told me they were done shopping at the market and went a few blocks further to check out some big dress sale at a local shop. They requested we pick them up there when I was done at the coffee shop. I settled my tab with the kitchen but didn't see Rico anywhere around to offer my thanks and say goodbye.

With my box of books in hand, we made our way down the street to the Impala. I was happy my car was still in the shade, it had to be 90° and as humid as a wet diaper. We crept through the crowded market streets trying not to run anyone over and found a great parking spot under a huge tree near the dress shop. Our women were nowhere in sight but there were plenty of others to ogle.

I reached into my cooler bag and retrieved two cold beers. The expression on Willy's face said it was love at first sight. To kill the time, I decided to tell him what Rico said to me about his theory on a serial killer. Watching him attack the beer, I figured he'd finish it before the perspiration on his forehead dried. He listened intently and didn't speak until I was done.

"Wow. You think he can really remember all his customers and when they were there? Seems impossible to me, but the serial killer thing kinda makes sense...you think?"

I waited to feel the cool beverage sliding down my throat before answering. "As far as his memory goes...yeah. I'm the same way with faces and most names, but some have faded through the years. I'll remember someone for no reason but then bump into them one day and have a brain fart trying to recall their name. Shit, I can even tell you some dirtbags birthdays."

"I hear ya...my brain farts constantly, probably more than my ass. So, where does that leave us with trying to pin down a suspect? There's a million people around here on market day."

"Yeah, it's like trying to find a single piece of hay in a haystack."

Willy eyed me as if I was speaking Chinese. "That doesn't make much sense, Edmundo." Besides a few locals, he was the only one who called me that.

I placed my beer can in the cup holder between our seats. "Bad analogy I suppose. What I mean is we know the killer is a piece of hay...one of many in the stack...yeah, you're right...that's stupid. But you know what I mean. He, or she, is here somewhere...possibly today if Rico is right. Trick is to narrow it down somehow. Is the killer one of the vendors, or a stranger blending in with the crowd?"

The big man tilted his beer can completely upside down trying to get the last drop. His sad eyes said it all. I tilted my head toward the cooler and told him there might be another one inside.

"I say it's a vendor, someone in the perfect position to sit back, watch people and select his next unsuspecting victim. They're only in town for the day so he does the deed and moves on."

I nodded. "Now you've got it, buddy. It's called deducing and elimination...you should have been a detective."

We clinked our beer cans just as the women exited the dress shop.

CHAPTER THIRTY-TWO

The P.I. Guy

Katie got a text from Sticks as I pulled up to the gate at Willy and Wanda's place. Wanda lingered to enjoy the air conditioning while Willy unloaded their groceries from the trunk.

"Sticks wants to know who's going to the beach table...she's got important news for the murder club."

My wife turned to me for approval. I shrugged. Wanda thanked me for the lift and said they'd be there. Katie returned the text and I drove the few blocks home. Another afternoon at the beach, two in the past week. If that continued, I'd ruin my reputation for abstinence. Checking the dashboard clock, I was relieved there would be time for my nap...I had priorities.

Katie passed on the text message from Sticks to the rest of the group. The phone was her domain, mine never left my suitcase the whole time we were in Mexico. I made it clear to friends and family back home they could email or catch me on Facebook. I hated being a slave to my phone when I worked and really didn't care to have one in retirement.

I didn't feel like writing so I did a bit of editing instead. About half-way done, it was coming along well and I was happy with it.

My brain was sluggish and lacked the ability to be creative so I killed time playing solitaire on Katie's iPad, gearing down for my afternoon nap.

She caught me leaving the bedroom after the snooze and asked if I'd set an alarm. Before I could answer Katie said, "You sleep for forty-five minutes, exactly...it's just like in the morning when you're always up at the same time. How do you do that?"

A bit groggy, I shrugged and headed to the bathroom to relieve my bladder. "My internal clock, I guess. What time are we heading to the beach?"

"Whenever you're ready, baby. I already packed your beer and water."

"You're the best...I knew I didn't marry you just for sex. Who's all going?"

"Most of the group...Helen's working at the shelter and Sticks says she doubts Bruce will come. She's been texting me like crazy...says some guy was there questioning them, but she'll wait to fill us all in at the beach. Oh, and GP's not going...Helen said he's been in bed most of the morning. His back again."

Trudi and Rudi were sitting at our table with Sticks when we got there. Katie and I hadn't even sat down yet when Trudi started. "Did you hear about the private investigator going around town questioning everyone about the missing girl in Barra?"

Sticks gave her a dirty look, pissed Trudi stole her thunder. She opened her mouth to interject but Trudi rambled on without pause.

"Some ex-military guy who hunts down victims of human trafficking. But he never mentioned Amigo or the teacher. Does anyone know who the other woman was that they found in the lagoon?"

She covered three more topics in short rapid-fire sentences before anyone could answer the question, as if she didn't have time to hear a response. Rudi stared off into space, his eyes glassy and red and fixed on the horizon. If anyone needed good weed, he was the guy to ask. Word was, he knew the best dealers in town and wasn't afraid to buy from them. Somewhere around seventy years old, I'm sure he smoked it for medicinal purposes. Every day.

When Rudi got up and wandered off toward one of the beach restaurants Trudi followed, continuing her news broadcast as she walked away. Sticks' face was red. She was obviously holding back from spewing the four-letter expletives hanging on the tip of her tongue. The rest of us exchanged raised eyebrows and rolling eyes, and eventually broke out in laughter.

Sticks relaxed and filled us in on the stranger who came to her door asking for Bruce. He introduced himself as John Smith and said he was representing the parents of Samantha Adams, the young woman who went missing in Barra de Navidad. She said Bruce was still 'in a mood' and was reluctant to answer any the man's questions.

Smith was interested in the other disappearances in town and wanted to know how or why Bruce wasn't one of them. When he mentioned Amigo, Bruce lost it and told the man to get out of their apartment. The PI didn't push it and did as was requested. Sticks said she showed Smith out and chatted a bit more with him outside, apologizing for Bruce's attitude.

He told her he was ex-military and retired, now a private investigator for missing persons from the US. Smith said he had experience in tracking down women who'd been sold into human trafficking rings this side of the border, and that he also negotiated with kidnappers where certain victims were held for ransom.

I spoke up. "That's big business in Mexico City...or at least it used to be. Companies put huge insurance policies on some of their executives for just that reason...to pay off their abductors. Does Smith think the Adams girl was kidnapped for ransom or that she's been sold off to a human trafficking ring?"

Sticks shook her head. "He didn't say for sure either way, he mostly asked questions. When I asked if he knew about Jorge, he barely acknowledged the name and changed the subject. I think he's aware of him but maybe didn't want to tip his hand with what he knew."

I reached up and adjusted the umbrella to keep the sun off me. Big Willy cut in. "That's what cops do...keep their hand close to their chest and ask questions instead of answering them. Right, Edmundo?"

I nodded. "Right, detective. He sounds like a professional who the family hired after authorities did nothing and treated Mr. Jorge like he's royalty. I've read about these guys and seen a couple movies on the topic. They usually have lots of money and teams of experts backing them up. Maybe Samantha's daddy is somebody important back home with the cash to make something happen down here.

CHAPTER THIRTY-THREE

Theories

What is it they say about opinions and assholes? It was like that with our murder club and theories. Everybody had one. Because of the visit from John Smith, Sticks was now convinced Jorge was our killer. Trudi and Rudi weren't members and they'd wandered off so any opinion they might have didn't matter.

Even though GP wasn't there, he was adamant Amigo was the murderer. Helen hadn't made her thoughts on the matter clear, although she had suspicions about Amigo because of Coco's strange reaction to him. Like she often did with her wardrobe, Katie changed her mind every time the wind shifted.

Big Willy still believed we had a killer crocodile on the loose. Wanda said she wasn't sure but with the new information on Jorge, she was leaning that way. Tequila Tommy joined our table around the time Trudi and Rudi left. He said the problem may be bigger than we thought and told us an old man was missing from La Manzanilla.

Discussion broke out around the table whether or not that occurrence should be included since the beach town was about thirty minutes away. It was somewhere we went every couple of weeks for a change of scenery and sustenance. Willy jumped on the bandwagon mentioning the huge crocodile farm there and how old 'Carl' kept pushing his way under the fence and onto the beach.

Carl is was the biggest croc I've ever seen, about the size of a Volkswagen minivan. There's enough skin on his body to supply the whole town with shoes and purses. If he was a man-eater, he could easily stuff a small person inside of him. Doing the boardwalk tour there, I once watched Carl being fed whole chickens. He snapped them up, like I do with popcorn.

Tommy, always the gamer, thought we should start a pool and bet on who the actual killer was. Willy wanted to know if it would only be for humans because he wanted Carl the croc on the list. I reminded him Melaque was a long walk or swim for his pick.

As far as I was concerned, the jury was still out. Who could say for sure there was only one killer, and if the others missing were actually dead. Not everything was always as it seemed. Someone once told me not to believe anything I heard and only half of what I saw. That proved to be true many times throughout my life.

We had picked up a pile of spare ribs earlier in the day and planned a barbeque that evening. I suggested we continue our conversation then, when more of our murder club were in attendance. Hearing about it for the first time, Tommy was put out that he hadn't been invited for dinner. Katie told him not to worry, that we had lots and he and Louise were welcome to come.

CHAPTER THIRTY-FOUR

Fishing

If I hated anything at all in life, it was getting up before dawn. Opening my eyes before the birds just wasn't in my DNA, but Morty booked a fishing trip with his buddy the police chief, Alfonso Alvarez. I never understood why men think they have to get up early to catch fish. Is it because they are still sleeping and like to have breakfast as soon as they wake?

My headlights caught Morty sitting on the bench in front of his bungalow. Being a daylight driver while south of the border, I couldn't remember the last time I had the headlights on. Driving at night in Mexico was not my idea of fun. There were way too many obstacles on the road or shoulder, just waiting to be hit or run over. Pedestrians in dark clothing, motorcycles with no lights, and even one idiot we saw with a LED bar duct-taped to his front grill.

Not one to let Morty think I was afraid of the dark, I drove to the pier in Barra de Navidad. Chief Alvarez and his brother-in-law, who owned the boat, were waiting for us. The craft sat in a pool of black ink. I am always amazed at how calm the water is in the morning. Some called it morning but dark means night to me.

As I climbed on board Morty introduced me to the chief. The man extended his right hand to greet me and gave me a beer with his left. The only other time I could recall cracking a beer at that time of day was when I had been up all night. But in most of rural Mexico, beer is safer than water if it's not in a sealed bottle. So, when in Rome...

Alvarez introduced the skipper but I immediately forgot his name. Captain sufficed so that's what I called him. He spoke to his his brother-in-law in Spanish and only smiled and said, 'Si' when we said anything in English. It was safe to assume he wasn't bilingual. It reminded me of a time in Victoria when we went to Chinatown for Dim Sum. I asked if the dumplings were pork or shrimp and the server simply smiled and said, 'yes'.

Morty and Alvarez started a conversation but were soon drowned out by the engine noise. Either the captain was in a hurry to get us to his favorite fishing hole or he wanted to show off the vessel's power. The bow was so high above the horizon I don't know how he saw where we were going. Still half asleep, I leaned back in the stern and enjoyed something I missed sorely since being in Mexico. A cool breeze.

There was nothing but ocean and a charcoal-colored sky in front of us. Shades of red and orange crested the water in the east. It reminded me of artwork we did in grade school, where you drew all over paper with different colored crayons and covered it in black. Then we scraped away the black wax into whatever shape we wanted, to reveal on our multicolored masterpiece.

The cold beer tasted pretty good, but it sloshed around in my empty stomach as we rode waves resembling a roller coaster. Luckily, my thoughtful wife made me a couple of breakfast burritos to take on the excursion. I wasn't awake enough to eat them before leaving the apartment but our journey to the horizon seemed the perfect opportunity.

The captain saw me and said something to the chief, who told me lunch would be served on board. Obviously, the man didn't know me and my stomach. Food was my secret to staying half-sober during drink fests. Besides, didn't he know breakfast was the most important meal of the day? Checking the meat locker that hung in Morty's lap, I had to assume he never missed many meals.

Figuring I needed another beer to wash down my burrito, the chief got up and reached for the cooler. The water may have been calm at the pier but our rolling waves became man-sized swells, one of them almost sent Alvarez face-first into the wheelhouse. He regained his sea-legs and shot the captain a dirty look, as if he did it on purpose. I graciously accepted another beer, having dumped half the previous one overboard when nobody was looking.

Finally, the captain let up on the throttle and the engine's roar calmed to a purr. The bow dropped down, offering an unobstructed view of absolutely nothing. If our skipper had found his fishing hole, I have no idea how. GPS? As it turned out, the break was to set up fishing lines and downriggers.

Morty and the chief had been shouting at each other over the engine noise since we left shore, trying to carry on a conversation. Turns out the Mexican cop was reminiscing about his visit to LA where the two men met at the police convention. I could tell he was proud of his heritage when he reminded us that California used to be a part of Mexico.

I gave Morty the look, signaling him it might be time to question the chief and get the inside scoop about what was going on in Melaque. My wide and wise friend paused in thought for a second, then retrieved a bottle of tequila from his lunch box. He answered with his eyes, saying we needed to lube and loosen the man up some more.

Glad I had a food base in my stomach, we each did a shot of tequila. They were the size of doubles but half of mine missed my mouth accidentally on purpose. All business, the captain ignored the boozers on board and readied our lines. I was curious as to what exactly we were fishing for and asked Alvarez. He said, "Big fish."

CHAPTER THIRTY-FIVE

The Catch

I checked out the boat while the captain got our lines into the water. I don't know much about sea-going vessels but it seemed adequate. When the chief mentioned big fish, I couldn't help but think about the movie, Jaws, and wondered if our boat was big enough. It was similar to other water craft I'd seen in the area and even had a portable thing for number two situations. Real men always pissed overboard.

The chief suggested another shot of tequila before we started trolling and I obliged by tossing mine back, missing my mouth again. From his angle he was none the wiser and I kept my wits about me. Morty went on offence and asked Alvarez directly, what was going on with the Melaque and murder investigations.

The chief momentarily lost his balance when our captain dropped the engine into gear. He talked in circles, blaming everyone else but his own people for what he called a political cluster-fuck. According to him, his men tried to question Amigo, but he was plucked from their custody and dragged off by the Federales.

He also said they tried doing surveillance on Jorge once, in the hope they'd collect some kind of evidence that could justify bringing him in for proper questioning. He rolled his eyes and laughed. Morty and I exchanged a quick glance, we knew exactly what 'proper questioning' meant in Mexican terms.

I asked, "What about his cartel protection?"

"Politics." He answered. "The governor's getting heat from the Americans about the missing white woman and he tells us not to worry about the cartel. Like many other elected officials, he was put into office by the same criminals who are protecting Jorge. His fate will be decided by whomever owes the other a favor. That's how it works, always has."

I nodded. Morty said, "It's the same everywhere, chief, it's either who you know or who you blow."

We all laughed. Morty's expression suddenly changed. I thought he was having a heart attack but his fishing rod bent in half and the line was dragged out to sea. It looked as if he snagged Moby Dick. The veins in his neck bulged as he tried to control his line. The captain told me to bring mine in to avoid a crossover. By the look on Morty's face, I couldn't tell if he was enjoying himself or in severe pain.

It was difficult to tell who was going to win, the big man or big fish. The chief was distracted by his phone ringing. He grabbed it and considered answering, but was totally engrossed in the action onboard. It stopped ringing and Morty continued his battle. His arms were shaking and sweat poured off his head like rain off a metal roof. I wondered if I could do any better in his situation.

The captain shouted instructions and the chief translated, both men yelling at the same time. Morty was tiring. Then a huge fish broke the surface and leaped into the air. It flipped and wiggled, trying to throw the hook. I'd only seen them mounted on walls but it looked like a huge sailfish to me. I turned to Alvarez who confirmed my suspicions. "Si, a sailfish...maybe big enough to keep."

When I glanced back at the captain he was on the radio, pointing to the action off the stern and yelling at whoever was calling. He shouted to the chief, waving him over to the microphone. I asked Morty if he was okay and how I could help.

His stare never left the water's surface. "A cold beer would be great...just dump it over my head. I don't want to lose this thing. Gotta be my biggest catch ever."

I'd been salmon fishing once, in the north-channel of Lake Huron, so I knew what it was like to land a big fish and the effort it took to bring it in. My chinook was less than half the size of the sailfish and it took me twenty minutes to get it in the boat. I thought my arms would fall off and they were sore for days.

The chief was loud and not happy with the radio call. He said they tried to call him, but couldn't get through to his phone. The district commander of the Federal Police was upset and wanted him back on shore immediately. Alvarez and the captain exchanged words; some four-letter ones came out in English. Our skipper was concerned about the fish on Morty's line. The chief was frothing at the mouth.

He snapped his head back and forth like Lind Blair in the Exorcist, pulled out his pocket knife, and charged Morty. I thought the worst for a second, but the chief grabbed the end of the big man's rod and cut the line.

Morty melted and looked like he'd just been dumped by his first love. Totally spent, as if he'd run the Boston Marathon, he turned to Alvarez. "Why the fuck did you do that...it was a catch of the century."

It appeared the chief had completely sobered up. "I'm sorry, my friend. I've been called back to shore...they've discovered many more bones in Laguna del Tule."

CHAPTER THIRTY-SIX

Buried Treasure

The resort was quiet when I got back. I found Katie playing with Coco on the living room floor and asked where everyone was. She said they went to check out the new bones found in the lagoon. Before I could ask, Katie said she didn't need to see that and volunteered to watch the dog for Helen and GP. "How was fishing?"

I grabbed a diet coke from the fridge. "Morty hooked a big sailfish."

"Really, how cool was that?"

"I don't know...the chief cut his line when they called him back to shore for the gruesome discovery. Guess there was nobody else to handle it."

"The pool guy says half the town is there...all kinds of cops and soldiers. He said his cousin was using a backhoe to dig a trench and install permanent drain pipes to maintain the lagoon's water level. That's where they found the bones...several bodies from what he said. I didn't think you'd be back for a while but you can probably find the rest of the murder club down there."

Curiosity got the best of me and I headed back out. Police had all the roads closed near the lagoon and I had to park several blocks away. I walked from there and use the beach access. It made more sense since I knew that's where they had to dig for the drainage pipe. Katie was half right; I think the whole town was there—tourists and locals alike. With all that had been going on, people were scared and curious at the same time.

The last time I saw that many uniforms was at a police funeral in Windsor when one of our own was gunned down. The Mexican authorities didn't need any crime scene tape, military and police personnel formed a human fence around the area. Being taller than most nationals gave me an advantage, being able to see over their heads. I searched the crowd for anyone else from the resort or our murder club.

A familiar face appeared in front of me. Dr. Lee was heading in the opposite direction, away from the action. I couldn't resist the opportunity. "What's up, Doc?"

He didn't get the Bugs Bunny reference. "Hello, Ed. I'm heading back home, they wouldn't let me get close enough to speak to my friend, the medical examiner."

"Any idea what's going on...I heard they found more bones?"

"Yes, the remains of many victims...buried deep in the sand on the edge of the lagoon where the water drains into the ocean. I managed a short phone conversation with my friend before they called him away. He said it's like quicksand there and the bodies stacked up as they sank lower and lower."

I tried to get another peek over his head. "Any idea on the number yet?"

He shook his head. "They're still digging but the wet sand keeps collapsing and falling into the hole...I've heard they've called in army engineers. My friend says the bones they've recovered so far are in the same condition...cleaned of any flesh. And there's an anthropologist on site whose preliminary investigation revealed some remains are much older than others, perhaps going back years."

Not sure what to do with that information, I wished the doctor well and let him go on his way. Moving forward into the empty hole he left in the crowd, I saw the Flintstones near their dune buggy, on the beach. I made my way over to them, cursing every step I took. Sand had found its way into my flip-flops. Fred and Wilma said hey, and how they came by earlier when the crowd was thinner, but the cops kept them at a distance.

Wilma said Victor was around somewhere, flying his drone over the scene trying to get video footage. He had to keep moving, afraid soldiers might shoot his machine out of the sky. Fred was a hair taller than me and I asked him what he was able to see. He said if I needed to pee, I should go in the bushes nearby. Nobody would be looking in that direction.

I thanked him and climbed up onto their buggy to see over the crowd. Fred told me I didn't need to drive; the bush was only fifty yards away. Chief Alvarez was standing near the hole with other uniforms and a few suits. Morty was nowhere in sight and I wondered if he'd heard any more after I dropped him off.

From my lofty vantage point, I was able to see some bones laid out on tarps near the hole. It was impossible to tell how many bodies there were or if they were male or female. I wondered if poor Gary was among them.

CHAPTER THIRTY-SEVEN

Mr. Smith

John Smith had been in town a week already, eyeballing and surveilling Jorge on two separate occasions, but found him doing nothing out of the ordinary. He wasn't hard to track down since most the taxis in Melaque and Barra de Navidad usually hung out in designated cab stands. The Zocalo, or main-square was the base of operations for the fleet of yellow taxi cabs.

The drivers congregated on park benches in shade near the dispatch office, awaiting their turn at a fare. Anybody shopping or dining downtown, could easily grab a cab there instead of trying to call and waiting for one to show up. Their standard answer by phone was, 'Cinco minutos', which could mean anywhere from five minutes to an hour.

Many snowbirds who used taxis in Melaque, stuck with their own drivers for more dependability. Before bringing our car to Mexico, we used a guy named, Juan. He had a clean and air-conditioned cab, and was always punctual. Smith figured that was the case while following Jorje around town. It appeared he had 'regulars', such as the kids he picked up going to and coming from school.

The PI hadn't caught Jorge committing any criminal activities or chasing women yet, mostly because the hack worked the day shift. At night, cab #69 was parked in front of a printing store. The suspect had an apartment upstairs. Smith didn't think Jorge was all that good-looking. He had a pockmarked complexion, neatly shaved goatee and black hair, slicked back with too much styling gel. Maybe women found him attractive because he resembled the actor Edward James Olmos.

From a distance, Jorge appeared to be somewhere between 35 and 45 years of age. Perhaps Samantha Adams had daddy issues and saw her father in her lover. Smith liked to work an investigation from the outside in. He kept his target at a distance while he interviewed Samantha's friends and other people in town who had disappeared and reappeared.

The American heard there were more than a few, some with foggy memories or none at all. Like a guy they affectionately called, Amigo, who'd recently been arrested for murder. To be sure, Smith checked for any links between him and Samantha Adams. Other than the fact Amigo collected beer bottles, there was nothing.

Like all good investigators, John Smith relied on confidential sources for privileged information not available to the general public. In his case, he reached out to a federal police officer he'd met in the military. He worked at a border interdiction training camp focusing on drug smuggling and human trafficking. With Jorge's supposed cartel connections, Smith hoped the Adams girl hadn't fallen victim to the latter.

Interviews with so-called friends of Adams were useless, mostly other young tourists who were more interested in the next good party. The only person offering anything useful was a maid at the apartment building where the Adams family stayed. She was around Samantha's age and got talked into going out with her one night.

The local woman said it was a one-time deal since she had no use for the American woman's circle of friends, one of which was Jorge. She told Smith the cab driver had access to marijuana and cocaine and plied young women with drugs and alcohol in night clubs in Barra. On another occasion, Samantha had the maid lie for her, having her parents believe she spent the night with her instead of Jorge.

Smith interviewed a bartender at one of the nightclubs Samantha frequented. The man had no problem talking about the young woman but he balked at discussing Jorge. He mentioned how the taxi driver was 'connected' and it was stupid for anyone to talk about him. The man grew wiser with the C note that Smith left on the bar for his two-dollar beer.

The bartender said Samantha was Jorge's seasonal flavor. That he found himself a younger and good-looking tourist every season, purposely selecting naïve Americans or Canadians who liked to party. Before Smith left the bar, the man wished him luck and said Samantha Adams wasn't the first of Jorge's playmates to disappear.

Meat Lovers

The commotion on the beach at the lagoon carried on into the evening, when the military set up lights to continue their investigation. I struggled to recall any incident in Windsor that had garnered so much attention. Perhaps the plane crash over the east end of the city that happened on my second day of training, walking a beat downtown.

A marked police car roared to the curb and waived me and my training officer inside. It was the fastest I'd ever driven across the city, blowing red lights and weaving in and out of traffic. Dispatch sent every cop working that day. Two single engine planes collided mid-air and fell to the ground in a residential neighborhood. Neighbors called in to report debris such as an airplane wing sticking out of their garage roof.

The scene was surreal. Police and firefighters scrambling to search the wreckage and put out fires on a burning fuselage. Residents came up to us with pieces of aircraft that landed in their yards. It was a miracle no one was hurt by the falling debris. Occupants of the two airplanes didn't fare so well. It was my first experience seeing dead bodies.

The crowds thinned out as the day dragged on at the lagoon, the methodical collection of evidence in such an investigation wasn't enough action to hold their attention. Having been there and done that before, I bailed early and returned to the resort. A few of the others had already returned and we chatted about the big event.

Our conversation was interrupted by my continuous yawning. It had been an early morning and interesting afternoon. Before the neighbors thought they were boring me, I excused myself and went for a nap. Katie was still dog sitting Coco, patiently waiting for Helen and GP to come home. She looked like she was having too much fun and I told her not to get any ideas. A cat at home was enough.

An hour later, I was refreshed and ready to rock. My growling tummy steered me toward the fridge. I grabbed two pepperonis and a diet coke, and took my laptop out to the patio. Not sure if I was in the mood to do any writing, I checked my various email and social media accounts. There was a message from Morty, who wanted to meet for breakfast. I agreed to meet him.

The next morning, I walked to a beach restaurant for breakfast. It wasn't far enough away to get my heart rate going so I normally continued the walk after loading up on my favorite foods. Morty was at our usual table where we could both sit with our backs to the wall, a habit we'd picked up from our years on the job.

I grabbed the glass of ice water waiting for me. "Thanks, you're getting to know me."

"Yeah, you're the only cop I've ever known who doesn't drink coffee."

"Mom always told me it would stunt my growth."

Morty rubbed his belly and we both laughed. "Quite the show down at the lagoon yesterday, hey?"

"A regular circus...seems someone has finally taken notice and our little town is now on the map. Did you see your buddy, the chief, there? I wonder if they smelled the booze on his breath."

"Yeah, I saw him but couldn't get close enough to talk. The military did a good job of keeping everyone back. We're just simple citizens now, Ed, no more badge power."

The waiter showed up at our table with a meat lovers' skillet for me and a ham and cheese omelet with side of bacon for Morty. He told me he'd be right back with my diet coke. I smiled. "Wow, you ordered ahead for us?"

He eyed me as if I just asked if he was gay. "Funny. I thought maybe you called ahead because they're so slow here?"

I returned his puzzled stare. "No...I don't even know the phone number. Are we that predictable? You're fucking with me, right? I was surprised by your message on Facebook...we're not even 'friends'."

Morty looked like he just let loose a wet fart. He shouted for the waiter and waived him over. "Amigo...why did you bring us this food?"

"Is something wrong, senior?"

"No. But we never ordered it."

The young waiter smiled and pointed to a man sitting by himself in the far corner. "Your friend over there, he order for you."

CHAPTER THIRTY-NINE

New Friends

The stranger laughed. He picked up his coffee and walked over to our table. Obviously at a loss for words, our mouths hung open wide enough to catch passing seagulls. Grabbing the back of a chair with his empty hand, the new face in town asked if he could join us.

Morty broke the silence. "Well, sir, if you're good enough to buy us breakfast then you've already paid for your seat."

The man sat down. Before I could pepper him with questions, he introduced himself. "I'm just screwing with you guys, seeing if you have a sense of humor. My name is John Smith."

I laughed. "And I'm Tom Jones."

Already digging into his breakfast, Morty almost choked on a piece of bacon.

"No, seriously guys...I've taken jabs my whole life. My brother is Bob, sister Jenny, and my dad was Joe...what can I say...my parents lacked imagination? Let me explain while you guys eat...go ahead, before it gets cold."

I shrugged and obliged. "Aren't you eating?"

"Already did...not bad for a Mexican beach town. Great bacon. Anyway, I'm in town looking for and trying to get information on Samantha Adams, the young woman who went missing in Barra."

Morty used a gulp of coffee to wash down a piece of toast. "We know who she is...not the only person who's gone missing lately. What's your interest?"

Smith went on, explaining he worked for her family and how it was one of the side jobs he did to make money. Still chewing on unanswered questions along with my eggs, I asked why he sought us out, how he knew where to find us, and what we ate for breakfast. He smiled and said it was one of his many talents.

"I'm sorry gentlemen, I do my homework. It's a small town and I've already talked to lots of people...many of whom know you two and what you previously did for a living. And I respect that...thank you for your service."

Morty wiped both corners of his mouth with a napkin. "Wait a minute, Mr. Smith, exactly how did you set this meeting up...with a social media page that I don't even have?"

He chuckled to himself. "I confess...just one of those talents...I'm good with computers, something I picked up in army intelligence, after a stint with the Phoenix PD. Once a cop, always a cop, right?"

I answered. "I guess that explains a few things. Army intelligence, cop, private investigator? You're a jack of all trades."

Smith held up his empty coffee cup, trying to catch the waiter's attention. "Guilty as charged. And I'm sorry to approach you guys this way but I know how receptive cops can be when someone they don't know tries to interrogate them."

Morty pushed his plate out of the way and crossed his arms on the table. "Is that what you're doing, John, interrogation us?"

Smith chuckled again. "Man, you've still got the moves, detective...move in closer to get more intimate, change your posture to let me know you're serious. I heard you were quite good in your day.

And you too, Ed. But you guys are retired now and not as many doors are open to you for your investigation."

I asked, "What makes you think we're investigating anything?"

He cleared his throat. "C'mon guys, the murder club?"

Morty and I exchanged glances, returning our attention to John Smith. I pushed my plate aside and mimicked my buddy's posture. "What about it? Realizing my reply sounded too defensive, I continued. "It's just a hobby for us retired folk in town...gives us something to do when we're not day drinking or napping."

"I didn't mean any offense, guys, I think it's a great idea and I'm hoping we can help each other...share information on what we know about the missing and murdered?"

Morty and I checked each other, nodded in unison. He answered. "Why the hell not, what exactly do you want from us?"

Smith scanned the horizon for good measure, before returning his gaze to us. "Well, when's your next murder club meeting?"

CHAPTER FORTY

Six Pack

With a pound of frozen mini lobsters in the freezer, Katie spread the word throughout our murder club it was shrimp night. She planned to start the shindig at happy hour with her famous bacon-wrapped, cheese-stuffed shrimp. Everyone else jumped on the band-wagon, offering shrimp in garlic butter, coconut shrimp, tempura shrimp, and peel and eat shrimp...all to be served throughout the evening as appetizers.

The mayor and sheriff were reluctant to have a stranger joining us for the club meeting, until he showed up and they got a look at him. He was younger than the rest of us, I guessed somewhere between forty-five and fifty. Smith had walked over from where ever he was staying, working up a sweat in the ninety-degree heat. He plopped his small cooler onto a table while I made the introductions.

Our new friend seemed distracted while trying to commit every-one's name to memory. He kept glancing at our pool, wiping perspiration from his brow. I knew exactly what he was thinking. "Go ahead, John, the water's great." Smith discarded his sandals and peeled off his shirt.

Silence fell over the gang. Gasps from the women were followed by jealous mumbling by the men. Smith's tanned and wet skin glistened in the sunlight. He was ripped, with a six pack that rivaled Arnold Schwarzenegger's in his prime. It was as if we were all frozen in time, watching Mark Spitz take to the water for another gold medal.

Not to be outdone, Big Willy grunted to regain our attention. He sucked his gut in and puffed his chest out, giving us his best weightlifter's pose. He and I slammed together like pro football players do after a touchdown. I bounced back like an Indian rubber ball off a brick wall and almost fell backward into the garden.

Everyone laughed, but the women continued ogling John Smith. "What kind of a phony name is that?" Quipped GP as he turned to me. "Do you really think that's his real name, considering what he does for a living?"

I flipped my brow. "He says it is but do you really care. He's talked to a lot of people in town about what's going on and has connections way out of our league."

Katie had missed the original Smith show but tripped over a curb on the patio when she saw him climbing out of the pool. Luckily, she managed to hang onto her appetizer. "Wow, it's really hot out here...I think I need a beer to cool down."

Mesmerized while watching him towel off, Wanda asked Smith if he wanted something cold to drink. His gaze fell on his cooler. "Let me get it for you, John."

Helen scooped up Katie's appetizer and met him before he got back to the table. "Stuffed shrimp, John?"

The guys rolled their eyes and exchanged goofy expressions, attempting to make fun of their women. Morty walked in the gate, a welcome distraction from the new guy's performance. Noticing the women were oblivious to his arrival, he asked me, "Was our new friend swimming naked or something?"

"No, but he's put together a bit tighter than the rest of us old men in town. Check out the six pack...you ever have abs like that?"

Morty patted his stomach and chuckled. "Sure, but I've worked plenty hard to sustain this twenty-four-pack."

Big Willy overheard our conversation and lined us up in a row. He called out to the women and we all raised our shirts at the same time. GP shouted, "Look girls, three sperm whales!"

Sticks and Bruce walked in and she shielded her eyes. "What the hell is going on...looks like we've got some catching up to do."

One look at the Batman and I could tell he still wasn't himself. Tequila Tommy was right behind him. Katie's shrimp were disappearing fast so I grabbed another one and dipped it into my own creation, a garlic-mayo aioli. I hate cocktail sauce.

Morty introduced the private dick to the newcomers and Fred grabbed me by the elbow on the way to the bathroom. "All you guys having the same problem, Ed?"

"What are you talking about, Fred?"

"You know...getting an erection...performance problems?"

Willy leaned in, not wanting to miss what was coming when I asked. "Where did you get that idea, Fred?"

"From you guys...talking about sperm and the new guy's dick."

Willy stifled a laugh and offered Fred his serious face. "I can't speak for Ed, but my dick works just fine...when I haven't drunk too much tequila. Maybe you should ask Mr. Smith yourself."

I checked Fred's ears for his hearing aids. It must have been all the groaning noises the women were making at the time. Wilma was normally his translator but she'd gone inside to get her appetizer. Katie came over to me and asked if we should get the meeting started. Scanning the crowd to make sure we were all there, I noticed Smith talking to Bruce.

Going behind the bar to fetch myself another beer, Morty came up behind me. "Hey, didn't you say the PI questioned Bruce before?"

"He tried, but I don't think he even went to the door. Why?"

"It sounded to me like he was interrogating him when I walked by. Grab me a beer from that green cooler, will ya."

I handed Morty a Michelob Ultra, same brand I was drinking. "Cheers to fat guys drinking diet beer. Hey, here comes Smith...you can ask him yourself."

The private detective came at us as if he was on a mission. "Hey, why didn't you guys tell me about the mark on Bruce's neck?"

CHAPTER FORTY-ONE

"V"

John Smith's head swiveled from side to side, as if he was checking to see who else was listening. Before Morty or I could answer, he nodded toward our building. "Hey, Ed, why don't you show me around your place...Morty can tag along."

I glanced at the retired LA cop, he tilted his head and flipped his eyebrows up. Smith waited until we were out of earshot from the rest of the group before continuing. We stopped at the front entrance to my apartment. "You want more privacy?" I opened the door and we stepped inside.

"You guys know I did some time with Army Intelligence, right?"

Morty replied, "You mentioned it at breakfast." His brow was still lifted, folded like a drawn venetian blind.

Smith took a quick glance around my apartment—not to check out the furniture but to make sure we were alone. "There's nobody else here, buddy...you gonna tell us Oswald wasn't acting alone when he killed Kennedy?"

He sighed. "The rest of your club doesn't need to hear this, and with your backgrounds I trust you'll keep it to yourselves. I've seen things...at one desert military base in particular. Things I can't talk about. Top secret shit."

I continued. "So, you brought us in here to tell us you've seen things you can't talk about? I suppose you were stationed at Area 51?"

The PI sat on the couch, pulled a pillow into his lap and clung to it as if it was his favorite teddy bear. "We called it Paradise Ranch or Dreamland."

"You're shitting me...the government's been denying and downplaying that place for years, saying everything since Roswell has been an elaborate hoax or paranoia by conspiracy theorists. What exactly did you do there?"

Smith stared at the floor. "I can't really say but thousands of people work there and are flown in on government jets from cities like Vegas every day. Most of the stuff that goes on there has to do with technological advances in military aircraft and weaponry."

"Yeah, everyone knows that...it's out there now, with the congressional hearings going on and whistleblowers telling tall tales. You saying you were involved in that shit?"

He lifted his head and met my eyes. "You got any beer in here?"

I checked the fridge and grabbed one for each of them. Morty was still standing and downed half the beer in one gulp. He listened and never said a word.

"I never had anything to do with spacecraft or anything like that. My job was to gather information on alleged abductees and interview them to look for comparisons and see if their claims could be proved or disproved."

Morty sat down and finally spoke up. "Is that why you went at Bruce so hard...he never really claimed he was abducted or anything like that."

"I know, I know...but he has the 'V' mark on his neck. I've seen it before at the Ranch while doing interviews. The common denominator seems to be loss of memory...some short and others long term, depending on how long they were missing."

As someone who's always been interested in the unexplained, I asked. "So, what exactly is the mark and how did they get it?"

"That's the weird part...no one really knows. Even the medical experts can't agree. Some say it's blisters, a reaction to an allergen, and others think it could be an injection site or even a tattoo or bar code of some type."

Morty almost choked on a swig of beer. "A fucking bar code? Wow, you got X files on these folks? I'm sorry, buddy, this is some pretty wild shit you're talking."

"What can I say? Bruce has the same mark on his neck as other people that I've interviewed."

"I asked, "How many people are you talking about?"

"That's classified. But more than one...and I heard about the man here, the guy you called Amigo. One of my sources said the man's current whereabouts are unknown and it wouldn't surprise me if someone else like me is interrogating him about his mark and memory loss. Who knows how they handle that here, in Mexico?"

By the expression on Morty's face, I couldn't tell if he was curious or pissed. "So, Bruce has a mark and memory problems like other folks you've ran run into. That doesn't explain the bones and bodies they've been digging up around here. What about our man Jorje...you getting anywhere with him?"

Katie came in the door and walked into the kitchen. "Looks serious in here...I need to use the bathroom. You guys better get back out there if you want any more shrimp."

CHAPTER FORTY-TWO

Answers

The shrimp fest turned into a drunken game of Name That Tune with GP winning, as usual. My secret for buzz management is to keep putting food in my stomach to soak up the booze. Since the shrimp were long gone, I snagged a few desserts when Katie wasn't watching. The intake of all those carbs meant serious mileage for the next morning's walk.

The mayor went upstairs for another bottle of wine and she called down from the balcony, waving us all up to see something. Whoever was left standing made their way up and crammed into her and GP's apartment. She was watching the local news and turned up the volume to drown out the rowdy crowd.

The broadcast was in Spanish but we pretended to comprehend what was being said. I recognized the police chief standing front and center with other officials from various levels of government. There wasn't enough room to sit but we piled on top of each other and giggled like teenagers drinking Boone's Farm for the first time.

I couldn't understand a word they were saying but Helen translated when she wasn't shushing us. She said they were talking about the human remains discovered in the lagoon. Film clips showed footage of the area and one photograph of a set of bones neatly displayed on a tarp in what appeared to be some kind of warehouse.

The media release took place at Cihuatlan City Hall in front of a mob of anxious reporters. From what Helen told us, the big shot from the Federal Police with all the medals and gold trim on his uniform, said their investigation was now complete. Most of the remains had been identified and their families could now have closure for their missing loved ones.

The crowd started to rumble when he said aggressive crocodiles were responsible for the deaths of those who simply wandered too close to the lagoon. He laid it on even thicker by saying common food sources for the reptiles had been depleted by past overflows and measures were being taken to stem correct the problem.

When questions from reporters flew at him like bats leaving their cave, he turned the microphone over to the police chief. The top cop actually cowered, as if he really was being attacked by flying vampires. Doing his best to sidestep questions about the ridiculous crocodile theory, he answered a reporter who asked about the arrest of Amigo and if they believed he was responsible for the additional deaths.

Our gang sat quietly, watching the broadcast as if it was the first moon landing. Chief Alvarez was a master at political doublespeak and openly admitted to nothing, saying the matter was still under investigation even though the federal cop said it was concluded only moments earlier. Morty laughed out loud and called the chief an idiot.

More questions were asked about Samantha Adams and if her remains had been found. Alvarez stammered and stuttered and turned to the medical examiner, trying to pull him toward the microphone. The man stepped back and disappeared behind the wall of dignitaries. The reporters pressed forward, shoving microphones into the faces of speechless officials. Another man in uniform stepped up and said there would be no more questions.

They lost control of the shit show. GP laughed out loud and said it was the most ridiculous press conference he'd ever seen, and he needed a drink. With a bottle of tequila already in hand, he started pouring shots. Some of the gang had already filed out the door, heading back to the pergola on the patio.

John Smith was waiting for Morty and I at the bottom of the stairs. "There you have it gentlemen, it's official...mass deaths by killer crocodiles. Only in Mexico."

CHAPTER FORTY-THREE

Confused

The club meeting ended early, probably because the news broadcast put a damper on things. That was fine by me, I couldn't go as hard as I did in my younger days. Where I used to be the last man standing, I was now one of the first to hit the sack. Katie stayed up with the mayor for a nightcap but she wasn't too far behind me.

The flip side of going to bed early is getting up early, by seven or seven-thirty, which is unheard of for me back home. The bright side was I beat the heat wave that came over the town by nine-thirty, turning me into a wet noodle. Katie let me wake up before she spoke. She knows I'm not a morning person and don't like heavy discussion until I have my wits about me.

I was going through my email and social media accounts when she sat down across from me at our patio table. "Can I speak?"

Clearing the frog that was still hiding in my throat, I answered. "Yes, darling..."

"I'm confused."

"About what?"

She'd just washed her hair and had a towel wrapped around her head. I smiled. My wife is a pretty woman and at that particular moment she reminded me of Barbara Eden in I Dream of Jeannie. Her cute summer jammies completed the perfect cuddly but seductive picture in my head and made me want to pick her up and drag her back to bed.

"Well...about the murders and bodies and stuff...crocodiles, serial killers, poor Amigo...and Gary and the American girl. You were a police officer. Do you have any idea what's really going on around here? Should we be worried...my friends on Facebook think we're crazy for coming to Mexico and totally insane driving here. Now they're asking if we're okay because of all the news about the missing woman."

I thought about how to answer her question and concerns. She had plenty of reasons to be confused but I didn't fear for our safety in any way. The media always sensationalized things and blew it out of proportion, scaring the shit out of people. Especially the American media, which dominated our newscasts back home because of Windsor's border location.

"I don't know what to say, baby. Somebody bad is out there and is or has been killing people. In many cases, missing people are just victims whose bodies haven't been found yet. But I guess guys like Amigo and Bruce are exceptions to that rule."

"But didn't Amigo kill that retired teacher?"

I downed the rest of my morning glass of water and closed my laptop. "That's what the Mexican authorities say but it doesn't mean it's true. That's what trials and juries are for...if he ever gets that far."

"What do you mean?"

"Well, from what I've heard so far, Amigo is lost in the system somewhere...probably stashed in a cell until they think they can make their case against him. But its Mexico, Katie, things are done differently here. That's why we gringos don't want to get arrested in this country." I paused in thought for a second before continuing. "And I don't think anyone buys the aggressive crocodile theory."

She took the towel off her head and fluffed her hair with her fingers. "I hate washing my hair...now I have to blow hot air on me for twenty minutes. So, what about that Jorge guy...I heard you and Morty talking to John Smith when I came in last night?"

"He's a good suspect, I think. Smith's been on him but doesn't seem to have much yet." I remembered it was market day. "Aren't you going to the tianguis this morning?"

"I might ride my bike down there...why, do you need something?"

"Not really...I just remembered something the coffee shop guy told me about market day and I forgot to pass it on to Smith. Maybe I'll talk to him after my walk."

Katie got up and headed to the bathroom. "Where is he staying?"

"Good question. I don't know."

CHAPTER FORTY-FOUR

Missing Women & Cats

I walked in the direction of the market but zig-zagged up and down the side streets along the way for a change of scenery. Camera in hand, as always, I snapped a few images of unique doors I hadn't seen before. I walked by a good restaurant I'd completely forgotten about and made a mental note to stop there on my next breakfast out day.

On one street corner I spotted a missing person poster taped to a lamp post. It had a picture of Samantha Adams with the date she went missing, and requested that anyone with information as to her whereabouts to call the phone number below. Wondering if it was John Smith's number and not knowing where to find him, I tore off one of the little tags at the bottom of the poster.

When I made my turn to head back home I ran into Doreen, the cat lady, carrying a shopping bag of groceries from the market. We hadn't spoken in a while so I stopped to say hello. She put her bag down on the sidewalk, asked how I was doing and if I'd heard about the crazy crocodiles that were eating people.

Taking one question at a time, I said that my life was good except for the usual old age growing pains. As I started to give my opinion on the crocs she cut in and said how stupid the whole thing was and that the government was just trying to sweep the mess under the carpet—like the disappearance of her cats—which she tried reporting to the authorities, but nobody cared.

There it was, the cat abductions. Being as serious and polite as possible, I asked if any of her feline collection had gone missing lately. She said no but that the one was gone for two months recently and returned with its neck shaved where its collar had been. Doreen thought it very strange that someone would do that, leaving a row of blisters on the bare skin.

Taken aback, I used my sweat towel to wipe sweat from my eyes and forehead. How the hell was I supposed to answer a remark like that? Was she trying to say that her cat had the same marks as Bruce and Amigo, after having gone missing? Deciding to leave it alone, I simply agreed it was weird and I hoped the cat was alright.

She liked to mention strange lights in the sky whenever her pets went missing but I used the excuse I had to get home for breakfast so I didn't have to hear the story again. 'Walk, talk and dump' is something Katie taught me when she still worked for a living and when she wanted to get away from someone in the office. That's exactly what I did to Doreen.

Crossing the main square in town, I saw that the print shop was open. Needing some colored markers to make a welcome sign for friends coming to town, I went inside. On the way out, I bumped into Doctor Lee who was on his way in. We started a conversation in the doorway but moved outside to stand in the shade. Very few businesses in town have air conditioning.

After getting the pleasantries about weather and our retirements out of the way, I asked what he thought of the press release about the missing and murdered people in town. A very laid back and reserved man, Lee only scoffed and said it was very disappointing.

"Unfortunately, it is like that here in Mexico. Government officials say anything to make it look like they're doing something.

It's the reason I got into politics when I did. I believe in the truth and did my best to be an honest politician, if there is such a thing. There are were so many tradeoffs and favors you have had to make to get things done. I think the governor is is worried about tourism now that the American news media is is saying how dangerous our country is is with the white woman missing.

I asked if he'd spoken to his friend, the medical examiner. Lee said he saw him at the lagoon when they dug up all the bodies but he was on the sidelines with the other local officials who were held back by a line of soldiers. The ME told him the Federals took over the investigation, even seizing the human remains he was storing at the local morgue. Somehow feeling he needed to apologize for something, the doctor said he was sorry and went back into the store.

A row of fresh carnations at a roadside stand caught my eye on the way by so I stopped and grabbed a pot to add some color to our patio. Katie and I both love flowers, one of the reasons we chose the ground-level unit at the resort, where we were surrounded by greenery. It is a perfect retreat for me to write.

After my celebratory dip in the pool, my reward for the morning cardio workout, I used Katie's phone to call the number on Samantha Adams' poster. I got a computerized answering service that gave an option to call another number for specific information on the missing American woman. John Smith answered on the second ring.

CHAPTER FORTY-FIVE

Job Offer

The American PI suggested I meet him for lunch at a taco stand on the main square, where he was surveilling Jorge at the taxi stand. Needing to pick up a few things at the pharmacy downtown, I walked to the zocalo. Smith was sitting on an outdoor patio only a couple doors down from the drug store.

Proud of myself for my second walk of the day, I joined him at his table. He was sipping on a beer, with the remnants of a tortilla on a plate in front of him. "I thought you invited me to lunch...looks like you already ate."

"I was hungry. Want a beer...you look hot and sweaty?"

"It's ninety fucking degrees every day here, I'm always hot and sweaty. And I just ate but I'll order a pop when someone comes around."

"Just as well...the burrito wasn't the best and I hate corn tortillas."

I nodded. "I've eaten here before, you're right. I hate those too but it's next to impossible to avoid tortillas in this country." Turning toward the taxi stand, I asked, "Which one's Jorge?"

"The guy laying on the bench in the shade. It must be a slow day; he hasn't moved in hours. Honestly, I think he's sleeping one off from last night and he's missed his turn in line. Other taxis have been in and out but nobody's tried to wake him up."

The man I saw was forty-five, give or take, with greasy black hair, wearing a wrinkled short-sleeved shirt and jeans. His cab, number 69, was parked about a hundred feet away. "How long have you been on him?"

"Since nine, he appears to be on the day shift and was sleeping in his car when I got here. They must have to put in a certain amount of time here at the taxi stand. I lost him last night, in Barra. By the time I parked my rental and got out on foot, he'd disappeared into one of the clubs. It's tough trying to watch him by myself. You ever work surveillance?"

I waived at a waiter and ordered a diet coke. "Yeah, quite a bit, actually. A lot in narcotics, then some in the B & E squad and fraud...everything from a mobile spin to sitting in the back of a van all day and pissing in a bottle."

Smith chuckled. "I hear you. Better here, I guess, with cold beer and a bathroom available. How would you feel about helping me out?"

"What...with surveillance?" The waiter put my coke on the table.

"Sure, why not? I could really use an extra set of eyes...especially to try and watch the target around the clock. I think the only time he sleeps is when he's working...like now."

I dabbed my forehead with a wad of napkins and took a hit of pop. "Really? It's been more than a few years."

Smith held up his empty bottle, trying to get the waiter's attention. "I'm sure you remember how...sit in places like this, eat and drink. All your expenses would be covered. The client basically signed over a blank check to me, trying to get his little girl back. And you'd get paid in greenbacks, not pesos. Cash. Maybe your buddy, Morty, would be interested if you're not...you guys easily blend in with all the other gringos in town."

I considered my answer before verbalizing it. "Morty just turned eighty and I just started collecting my old age pension. Between the two of us we have enough knee, hip and back problems to keep a team of orthopedic surgeons busy for a month."

Smith laughed. He pointed to a long scar on the inside of his right knee, and another one on his left shoulder. "Like these? There's another one the middle of my back where I still carry a piece of shrapnel big enough to set off metal detectors at the airport. It's too close to my spine for them to fuck with it and I know when it's going to rain.

Look, Ed, it's not like you have to chase anyone and you can work your own hours...just enough to give me a break once in a while. You know how surveillance works...it's much easier to cover the target with a team. I could even cover a rental if we go mobile and you don't want to use your own car. What else do you have to do with your time?"

I finished off my coke. "Not much, really. My writing." I considered the offer. "Should probably run it by my wife."

"The job pays fifty bucks an hour. Cash"

I fell back in my chair. "I'm in."

CHAPTER FORTY-SIX

Monsters

Sundays were fun days. Katie and I would jump in the car and go for a ride up or down the Pacific coast to check out other beach towns. On this particular day, the Wonka's—Willy and Wanda (not really their surname) joined us for a trip to Manzanillo to grab some groceries and do lunch at a place called, Monster Burger.

Manzanillo is was a busy resort/port city of about 150,000 people, the largest place near Melaque. We went there to get better prices on food and booze, and visit well-known chain restaurants for a break from tacos. It's also a place to find ATMs' where you can withdraw large amounts of cash, unlike Melaque where machines are were often broken or empty.

The car ride is is about an hour. The last half being more scenic as you drive right along the ocean...you can can hear waves crashing on the beach. The city's resorts were a hot spot and attracted hordes of tourists before the gulf coast became so popular. Unlike Melaque or Barra de Navidad, you can still find an assortment of all-inclusive high-end resorts in Manzanillo. Katie and I spent a couple nights there the previous year to celebrate our wedding anniversary, a nice break from our sleepy little beach town.

The four of us chatted about nothing in particular on the ride but like many of our other conversations as of late, the murder club became the topic. Big Willy and I rode in silence up front, leaving the women in the back where they carried on their own conversation.

Katie breached the man-wall and directed a comment at me. "I bumped into my old taxi buddy, Juan. He said he saw you at a restaurant downtown with another man the other day. He wondered who the other guy was because he's seen him hanging around for no particular reason. Isn't that where you had lunch with John Smith?"

I checked the mirror to catch her reflection in the back seat. "Yeah, he was keeping an eye on Jorge, at the taxi stand. That's when he asked me if I wanted to help him with surveillance. I hope you didn't say anything about Jorge."

She leaned forward. "No, but he said something weird like 'they're probably watching one of our guys, everyone hates him but he's protected'. He never mentioned anyone's name but I remembered you guys talking about him being untouchable."

"That's interesting..."

Willy cut me off. "Smith wants you to do PI work with him? Surveillance?" He glanced my way.

I flipped my eyebrows. "Yeah, I guess. Said he's been watching Jorge but can't keep up to his around the clock schedule. Told him I'd think about it."

"Would you get paid?"

"That's what he said...plus expenses. The Adams's family is loaded and has given him free reign to do whatever it takes to get Samantha home."

Wanda spoke up. "I hate to say it, but she's probably dead and buried somewhere." She clipped Willy on the back of the head. "And don't even think about getting involved."

He responded. "Could be fun...how hard can it be, Ed?"

"Honestly, it's mostly sitting on your ass and trying to blend in to your surroundings while you keep an eye on the target. It gets more difficult if he's on the move, especially in a car. Smith said he'd cover rental expenses if I don't want to use the Impala."

Willy twisted in his seat to face me. I could almost hear the wheels turning in his head. Wanda clipped him harder and he decided not to speak. We drove around the grocery store parking lot trying to find a spot in the shade so my car interior didn't melt from the heat. As couples, we went in separate directions with our shopping carts.

After working up a thirst, we headed out in search of the Monster Burger. We'd all been there at least once prior with other friends. They served giant one-liter draft beers and burgers so big they're difficult to get your lips around them. I was blown away when I walked by the bar on the way to the washroom and saw them pouring bottled beer into our draft glasses. WTF? The others didn't believe me and had to see for themselves on the second round.

Willy waited until Wanda was a bit lubed up before he asked me again. "Hey, Ed, what'd you say Smith is going to pay for help?"

Wanda flicked a French fry at him. It bounced off his forehead and landed in his beer. I didn't bother to answer his question.

CHAPTER FORTY-SEVEN

Part-time Work

John Smith popped by our apartment after dinner that night. He looked beat and I had a good idea why he came over. "I know you're retired, Ed, and police work is probably the last thing you want to get back into, but I can really use some help with Jorge."

Katie washed dishes in the kitchen, while we sat and chatted on the patio. I offered him a drink but he declined. "Are you on him 24-7?"

He sighed. "Not really...like now...it's his nap time. He normally drives the taxi during the day, when he's busiest in the morning with the work and school crowd. Then he repeats the routine in reverse taking his regulars back home. After his nap he keeps the taxi in and around Barra where he caters to the nightclub crowd, a prime time for preying on drunken women.

"Jorge went to 3:30am last night. He was alone when I tucked him in. I'd like to spend all my time on him but I still have witnesses to track down and interview. It's getting late in the season and some of Samantha's friends have already headed back north. Have you given my job offer any more thought?"

I glanced through the patio door to where Katie was in the kitchen. It wasn't like I needed permission but technically Melaque was our winter getaway, something we did together. For the most part, I enjoyed doing surveillance when I was on the job but actually committing to something like that while enjoying my retirement was a different story.

"I can see you're dead on your feet, John. You said the family had deep pockets...can't they buy you some additional help?"

"They can and will, but good help is hard to come by. That's why I asked you, someone with experience that I already know."

"It's been a lot of years since I did anything like that."

Smith smiled. "What do they say about riding a bike? Besides, I heard you were good at it."

I returned a crooked smile. "How would you know that?"

"Think you're the only one who had sources and CI's? Your name popped up when a Secret Service buddy of mine ran you through their data base...something about an international fraud investigation involving Western Union?"

I remembered the case well, a six month, half-million-dollar investigation where the main target got off easy but was later killed by a Romanian crime syndicate. "Data banks eh, the information is there forever." I'd already made my decision but didn't rush to give Smith an answer. "How many hours a day or week are we talking?"

"Nothing too long or steady, Ed. I appreciate where you're at in life and I'm envious. A greedy ex-wife keeps pushing my full-time retirement date back. Maybe some daytime hours to see where he goes when he's not taxiing folks around. It would be nice to see who he's connected to. You could use my car or another rental...that Impala of yours doesn't blend in well around here."

I felt a presence over my right shoulder. Katie was standing in the doorway, behind the screen. "Go ahead and do it, Edmond, you know you want to."

CHAPTER FORTY-EIGHT

The News

I was in the pool for my usual after-walk cool down, when Helen came downstairs on her way to the animal shelter. We exchanged our morning pleasantries and she asked, "Did you see the news last night?"

Picking a fallen leaf from the water, I replied, "No, we can't understand a word they're saying...even Katie can't keep up when they're spewing Spanish that fast. Why, did we miss something important?"

"I know what you mean, my brain can't always work fast enough to translate. The governor's cronies were on, talking about the human remains recovered from the lagoon." She chuckled. "You wouldn't believe the crap they're telling people now...how wild boars could have attacked and torn people apart before leaving them for the crocodiles."

"What kind of bullshit is that?"

"Exactly. They consulted and quoted all sorts of experts...like forensic anthropologists and marine biologists to try and explain how other creatures in the lagoon could have eaten away and cleaned the bones or left teeth impressions. Obviously, it's all a ploy to appease tourists and locals alike."

I moved to the edge of the pool and grabbed my towel. "Wild boars eh, we see lots of those around town." We both laughed. "And you gotta wonder what other kind of flesh-sucking creatures are lurking in the lagoon."

Helen started to move toward the gate. "Maybe we need to call the club together later...I should be home before dinner. Hey, I saw John Smith here last night...anything new from him?"

She was already half out the gate and I waived her off. "Not much...I'll fill you in later."

My towel wrapped around my waste, I peered into the fridge to see what I could whip up for breakfast. Katie came up from behind me and reached under the towel. "Was that the mayor I heard you talking to outside?"

"Yeah, she wanted to know if we saw the news...something about wild boars dragging people into the lagoon, where crocodiles finished them off."

"Really? Should I be worried when I'm biking around there?"

I put leftover sausage and three eggs on the counter, and gave her my best 'did you really just ask that blondie?' look. Seeing that I was still dripping and making the floor wet, I headed to the bedroom to finish drying off. "I think your safe baby...just pedal really fast and outrun them."

Katie's phone rang. She answered and handed it over to me. "It's for you...John Smith."

"Hey buddy, what's up...did you hear about the wild boars running around town?"

"What? No, I was...wild boars...what the fuck are you talking about?"

"It was on the news last night...the governor's latest answer to the missing and dead."

"Wow. Hey, I really need to catch some z's...can you cover me for a few hours? Jorge's at the taxi stand right now and they don't seem very busy."

I looked over at Katie who had an ear open. She shrugged. "Okay. Can I wolf down my breakfast first?"

"Sure. Can you walk over...I'm plugged into a nice shady spot with a good eye. We'll just swap places when you get here. I'm in the white Toyota."

"Alright, give me about twenty minutes."

When I got downtown, I could tell right off Smith had surveillance experience. He was parked facing away from the target, almost a block away, using his mirrors to keep watch. Seeing he was fighting to keep his eyes open; I grabbed the driver's door handle without warning. With his attention focused on what was behind him, he was startled.

"Asshole...lucky I'm not packing...you might have got shot."

"I was just checking to see if you were awake or could see anything through those little slits. When's the last time you slept?"

Smith shook his head to clear the cobwebs. "I kinda dozed off a couple times, mimicking my target over there." He tilted his head toward the casually-dressed Mexican laying on a park bench. The bone-tired PI swiveled his head to see who might be watching, before he climbed out of the car. "It's all yours, Ed, I'll check back with you before dinner. You got your phone?"

"Yeah...first time I've had it out of my suitcase since we got here. I don't have a long-distance package but I think you can text me." I gave him my number, not knowing if we'd be able to communicate by phone. "Hey, where the hell are you staying?"

He was already walking away. "A place down the street, on the beach...Playa something or other. Good luck."

CHAPTER FORTY-NINE

Surveillance

Jorge was sprawled out on the park bench like he just finished a full-blown thanksgiving dinner. The thought of it made me glad I had time to grab breakfast before taking on the surveillance job. Still not sure how many hours I wanted to clock with my new gig, I was happy to help out Smith. When I took over, he resembled the walking dead.

The man was dedicated and I wondered exactly how much the Adams family was paying him for his services. He'd offered me fifty bucks US an hour, in cash. It's not like I needed the money but who can't use a little extra to blow on the finer things in life. Obviously, Katie would benefit from my cash influx so she didn't make a fuss when I accepted the job.

Her only remark was to be careful, a common suggestion to every police officer when he walks out the door. But Katie and I met after I retired so she never knew me as a cop, and she freely admits she would have been a basket case, worrying about me at work every day. It wasn't that way with my first wife, who was a civilian employee at police headquarters.

Calling on my past experience with conducting surveillance, I scoped out the area in search of another spot in case I was compromised or had to move for some reason. No matter where you park, there is always someone who might get suspicious seeing a strange man sitting in their neighborhood for hours on end. There was more than one occasion when I was on the job that I heard dispatch send someone to check out a suspicious vehicle.

It was hard not to reminisce and think about my days in narcotics. I remembered one occasion when we were staking out a crack dealer with an active file. Being new to the unit, I was partnered with a younger female. She was junior to me in seniority, but had made it to the drug squad first. The irony was I trained her rookie ass when she came on the job.

We were watching a townhouse in the west end projects when someone suddenly appeared at the passenger window where my partner was seated. I recognized him immediately—it was our target. He politely asked what we were doing there and if he could help in any way. My partner froze and stared straight ahead, as if pretending she was invisible and our guy couldn't see her.

He asked if we were police and I said yes—we were department of labor cops, checking up on the roofers working across the courtyard. Our crack dealer turned around to see the crew I pointed to. He spun back to us and scanned the inside of our car. The puzzled expression on his face told me there was a good chance he bought my bullshit.

We left our spot and drove around the other side of the projects to see if there was another vantage point. It made my day when I saw the fly-by-night roofers rushing to pack up their equipment. There was another time when a concerned neighbor checked up on me, parked in her driveway. I had assumed there was no one home. The woman was so happy I was watching the suspected drug house, she later brought me lunch.

Only an hour into my stakeout on Jorge, I remembered how boring it could be. When conducting surveillance with a team, members switch up positions to keep a fresh eye and look less suspicious. Flying solo, I didn't have that luxury. I grew drowsy and realized my normal nap time was fast-approaching. The sun had encroached on my shade, only adding to my fatigue.

My target was oblivious, probably dreaming about his next score. He couldn't have hoped for a better job, driving a taxi and picking up drunk women. Being my own boss, I decided to look for another spot. Instead of driving around and attracting attention, I got out to walk and get my circulation going. The stroll would keep me awake.

When I was with the B & E squad, I was part of a task force surveillance team with the Ontario Provincial Police. Working with their spin team, we targeted one particular suspect in the Town of Belle River. At one point the team leader followed our guy to a corner drug store. Instead of parking and keeping an eye, the veteran cop drove back and forth by the business. The suspect came out with a disposable camera and took pictures of our guy on his second or third pass by. Even I knew not to drive by any place more than once.

Walking around the outside of the main square, I could either see Jorge or his parked taxi cab, in between the trees. I popped into a variety store to grab a diet coke and bag of peanut M&Ms for the caffeine and sugar buzz. After spotting another place to park on the opposite side of the square, I headed back to the car.

Jorge hadn't moved when I drove by. A pigeon sat on the top rail of his bench but it's ass disappointingly faced the wrong way. There was no shady spot to be had but I parallel parked with the passenger side exposed to the hot sun. There was no breeze and I forgot to bring my sweat towel so I used the front of my shirt to wipe my face. I was far enough away to turn on the AC but it would only draw more attention.

Only in my new spot for a matter of minutes, I saw a commotion at Jorge's bench. Another man, perhaps his boss, yelled at him and waived his hands wildly, pointing towards his cab. Nap time was over. My target sat up on the bench and waived the other man off. He rubbed his eyes, stood up and shuffled over to his ride.

An elderly woman carrying two large grocery bags stopped at the rear passenger door of Jorge's cab and waited for him to come around and open it. He ignored her and climbed in behind the wheel. She was barely seated in the back seat, with her hand on the open door when he pulled out of his parking spot and turned onto the street that would take him right past me.

I used a newspaper Smith had left in the car to shield my face. Waiting for him to get a safe distance down the road, I pulled into traffic and followed the hack. Obviously, the object of tailing someone successfully is not to lose them. But if it means getting burned, then it's best to let the target go and pick him back up later. There were two vehicles between us when Jorje turned on the highway towards Barra. We called them shade.

Assuming that's where the fare was going, I was surprised when they turned left and headed into the barrio north of Melaque. Not being familiar with the roads in that area, I hung way back and pulled to the curb when the cab stopped to let the old woman out. Jorge made a three-point turn and headed back in my direction. This time I ducked out of site, figuring he wouldn't recognize my car.

I waited until he turned east on the highway, again heading toward Barra, before I made a U-turn and tried to catch up. Accelerating quickly to close the gap, I completely missed seeing the speed bump and bottomed out the front end of my car. It was a common occurrence in Mexico, where such obstacles are rarely marked.

Jorge had stopped in front of a restaurant on the main road in Barra de Navidad by the time I caught up. He was walking in the front door, when I found a parking spot. I was still deciding whether or not to shut the engine and AC off, when my target strolled out of the eatery carrying a plastic shopping bag. I wasn't close enough to get a good look but could see there was something of substance in the bag.

The taxi driver turned around and headed back towards the highway. I followed and he went towards Melaque. Once in town, he took the same road that leads to the main square and taxi stand. Figuring that was his destination, I gave him plenty of room. But I was wrong and Jorge turned down the first side street, heading west, away from downtown. When I came around the corner, he was stopped in front of a known drug house.

A young man came out the front door and Jorje handed him the shopping bag he picked up in Barra. The local went back inside his house and my target went around the block, heading back to the main square. He was pulling into his parking spot when I drove by. Someone called my name and I saw John Smith standing on the sidewalk nearby.

CHAPTER FIFTY

Rubbing Meat

"How do you know it was a drug house?" Smith asked while debriefing me.

"Because I go by there all the time on my morning walks and I've seen hand-to-hands on more than one occasion when I worked in narcotics...and one of our neighbors buys his weed there."

"They sell anything else?"

"I think so...I've seen all sorts of customers coming and going...some looked like meth-heads. If you're thinking Jorge's supplying them, he could be a middle man or just a delivery guy...like Skip the Dishes."

Smith laughed. "Doesn't really matter...I'm no closer to tying him to Samantha Adams' disappearance." He looked at his watch. "What are you doing for dinner...I'm buying?"

I glanced across the way to where Jorje was standing and chatting with another driver. "Katie's cooking tonight...steaks, I think. What about our target, who's gonna watch him?"

"A home-cooked meal would be nice; I'm so done with the local taco stands. And we can find Jorje later...he doesn't stray too far from his daily routine—at least he hasn't so far."

"So, why did you have me sit here in the hot sun all afternoon?"

Smith surrendered his shoulders. "A couple reasons: I have to show the client I'm putting hours in, and I was really hoping you'd change my luck and Jorge would do something out of the ordinary. You covered both bases." He smiled.

"I get it. Now you've invited yourself to dinner, we have to stop and pick up another steak." I put the car in gear and pulled away from the curb.

"Can you buy a decent steak in this town? I haven't had much luck in the restaurants here or in Barra."

I drove to the butcher shop and stopped by the side door. "They've got great meat in there...tell them you want the Canadian beef and they'll cut you what you want if you don't see anything you like in the display case."

"Aren't you coming in?"

"You said you were buying...my meat is at home."

John Smith wore a grin like a kid who'd just been given money to go buy ice cream. He returned to the car with a smile that said he just got a double scoop of his favorite flavor. I drove by and pointed out the drug house on the way home. He had his nose in the bag from the butcher shop and paid the house little attention.

GP was sitting under the pergola sipping on a beer and listening to music. He nodded and raised his can—an open invitation to join him for happy hour. I hollered to Katie and told her to put some clothes on, that we had company. She liked to run around the house naked at times but was fully clothed and greeted me with a kiss. I told her John was invited to dinner and he brought his own steak.

It sounded like half a cow when he plopped the bag on the kitchen counter. Katie opened the bag and took a peek. "Wow, that's a big piece of meat you've got, John." The words were barely out of her mouth when she realized what she just said. Katie blushed.

I grabbed Smith and I a couple beers from the fridge. "We're going out to join GP for happy hour. Can you do something with John's meat?" I couldn't resist and received a love tap on the bicep for my trouble.

Always the generous sort, GP asked if we needed a beer as we approached. I raised my can and said we had it covered. He always kept the community fridge under the pergola stocked for anyone who wanted to help themselves. I said, 'thanks anyway' and asked if he remembered Smith. He nodded and motioned to empty chairs across the table from him.

We sat down and GP personally greeted us. "Well, if it ain't Crockett and Tubbs, how goes the investigation?"

I answered while Smith worked on draining his beer can. "Slow as the service in a Melaque restaurant." That earned a laugh from GP.

"The princess tells me you guys are having steak tonight? I just happen to have a side of beef to throw on the Q if you don't mind Helen and me joining you."

"The more, the merrier...ain't that our motto around here?"

He looked at Smith, who had one eye peering into his empty beer can. "There's more in the fridge, young man. Help yourself."

Smith smiled, said thanks and asked if I was ready. I wasn't but agreed anyway and turned to GP. "We watched the cabbie for a bit today and caught him doing a dope delivery but not much else. Seems he sleeps a lot when he's not out chasing women and partying at night."

"Yeah, our murder club hasn't figured out shit either...not that I ever thought we would. Do you guys think Jorge is good for the Adams girl or any of the others?"

Smith sat down in his chair. "He's a player, no doubt, and a likely candidate but there's nothing connecting him to the others. Especially not the males...nothing there makes any sense. Unless he's a hitter for the cartel...but what's their motive in taking out tourists?"

GP nodded, took a sip of beer. "So, it's some other serial killer, man-eating crocodiles, or Ed's favorite...extraterrestrials." He laughed and slammed his beer can down hard enough to make it foam over.

I laughed with him. "It's all a bit comical, actually, except for the fact that real people are getting killed by someone or something else. The Mexican authorities are dragging their feet and making up bullshit excuses for what's happening...waiting for the end of tourist season when everything will just fade away.

Katie came out carrying a glass of wine and joined us. The sound of Helen's flip flops on the stairs meant she was coming too. She arrived with a plated appetizer in hand. Smith glanced at me, his eyebrows and corners of his mouth raised. It appeared he was enjoying our company so far.

We chatted about nothing in particular until GP, Helen and John reminisced about living in Atlanta at some point in their lives. Eventually, the topic of the missing and murdered came back around when Helen asked, "How's the case against the taxi driver going?"

As if rehearsed, all three men answered at the same time. "It's not." GP scoffed and got up to light the barbeque. Smith asked if there was anything he could do before dinner.

Katie answered, "I've already rubbed your meat, it's ready to go."

Helen giggled. "Do tell, Katie." They both laughed. Smith too, although it appeared he wasn't quite sure what to make of us old farts. What he did know was how to drink beer and he asked if he could have another. His phone rang and he stepped away from the table to answer it. The call was short and he appeared happier when he returned. I asked what was up.

"That was one of Samantha Adams' friends...she's been out of town but heard I was looking for information on Jorge and wants to meet in Barra, Sunday morning after church."

CHAPTER FIFTY-ONE

Identifying the Dead

I couldn't help but to think about Smith and his morning meeting when I headed out for my daily walk. My ass was late getting out of bed, after overindulging at the dinner party the previous evening. Trying to keep up to the young American man proved that I was no longer a champion beer drinker. Unlike wisdom, stamina and alcohol tolerance are two things that don't get better with age.

Taking the outside loop around town, I purposely walked by Dr. Lee's place to get any updates he might have. There were no signs of life at his apartment. I did run into Gary Hart's partner, Allison. She still wore a shell-shocked expression when I saw her heading into the gym. Not quite sure how to address her, I stuck to pleasantries and wished her a good workout. What else could I say to a woman whose man disappeared on a golf course?

Allison called out to me from inside the doorway of the gym and I turned to face her. She struggled to find the words but told me the authorities notified her that Gary's remains were not among those found in the lagoon. Without thinking, I asked what that meant. She burst into tears and went into the gym. I guess that was my answer.

It wasn't my breakfast out day but I swung by the restaurant anyway, thinking I might catch up with Morty. He was by himself in his usual seat, watching the pelicans dive-bombing for fish. I asked the waiter for a large glass of ice-water on my way by the kitchen. Morty nodded a greeting while his mouth was full. He soaked up egg yolk with his last piece of toast.

I sat across the table and waited for him to finish. "You ever wonder how those birds don't knock themselves out hitting the water like that."

He washed his last bite down with coffee. "Pretty crazy, ain't it? But they always seem to come up with a meal. Didn't know you were coming...I could've waited a bit."

"I'm good, got some leftover steak from last night to have with my eggs when I get home. Smith came over for dinner and taught me I'm not a heavyweight drinker anymore. How can a man eat and drink whatever he wants and stay in shape like that?" The waiter dropped off my glass of water.

Morty leaned back in his chair and burped. "Sorry." He patted his belly. "He obviously hasn't worked as hard as you and I at perfecting our physiques."

I chuckled. "There ya go. Hey, any news to report...haven't heard much since the big news broadcast. Seen any of those killer hogs around town?"

Morty laughed. "Can you believe that shit? We fed the media plenty of crap back in my day but that story was right out of a Stephen King novel."

"I hear ya. I just ran into Allison Hart...says they notified her Gary's remains weren't among those in the lagoon. She's still pretty broken up about it. Can't say I blame her."

The big man wiped his mouth with a napkin and held up his empty coffee cup for a refill. "Not knowing is the worst. I had family members of missing and murder victims in LA who would call me all the time hoping for any new information. Some went on like that for years...so sad."

"Can't say I ever dealt with anything like that directly. Hard to imagine what it would be like if it was my wife."

"Some learn to cope and carry on with their lives. Others never get over it...I've seen families completely destroyed. They all want closure but don't feel any better if and when they actually get it. I did hear a rumor authorities grabbed another transient and dragged him in for questioning. Maybe Smith can reach out to his sources and confirm the story?"

I was still perspiring and wiped my face. "I'll ask him...he's hired me on to help with surveillance on the taxi driver, Jorge. He's supposed to be meeting a friend of Samantha Adams this morning...she might have some info on him." I downed the rest of my ice water.

The waiter delivered Morty's coffee. He picked it up and sipped without checking how hot it was. After thousands of previous cups of joe, it didn't faze him. "Doing PI work huh, I did some of that after I retired...mostly checking up on cheating husbands. Good for you...making a bit of beer money."

On the final stretch home, I saw Sticks and Bruce walking in the opposite direction on the other side of the main drag. Not having seen them in a while, I wondered how Bruce was doing. Two tourist buses passed between us and they didn't see me. Katie usually kept in touch with the other women on Facebook or by text so I made a mental note to ask her if she'd heard anything from Sticks.

Maria

Being brought up a Roman Catholic, I remembered something the good Lord said about Sundays being a day of rest. So, even though I converted to atheism at some point in my life I still did my best to do as little as possible on church day. My idea of 'mass' on Sunday's was with Katie, when we had a Mid Afternoon Sex Session. Because of the short but sweet physical workout, I skipped my morning walk.

Instead, out of curiosity, I asked John Smith if I could tag along when he went to see Samantha Adams' friend in Barra de Navidad. Since Maria Cortez was the church-going sort and requested to meet after mass, I took the American PI to my favorite breakfast spot, Quetzal. It is in Villa Obregon, east of Melaque and on the way to Barra so it worked out well.

I recommended one of their specialty omelets but it seemed Smith was still in a fog from our steak dinner and he struggled with his decision. He'd completely polished off his first coffee before deciding on a meal. "You can't still be hungover...that was two nights ago."

He shook his head. No, I'm over that but caught some kind of stomach bug...I didn't eat anything unusual that I remember."

"Doesn't matter...us gringos catch everything that's going around, doesn't have to be food or water related. Could be anything else that's unsanitary around here. Funny how locals can eat fly-covered meat that's hung in a window all day and not get sick, but the wind blows a certain way and we're down for the count. We're too pampered...everything is sterilized, pasteurized or homogenized."

"You're telling me I shouldn't try the Melaque coffee on the corner with all the cows?"

I laughed. "I won't go anywhere near that place...walking by at eight-thirty in the morning, I see tourists shit-faced before their day even starts. Grappa and warm cow's milk...no thanks."

The waiter came and took our orders. Smith played it safe and ordered the same omelet as me, a flank steak with mushrooms and cream cheese. It came with a little fresh-baked bun, and sides of salad and home fries on the plate. All for half the price of anything back home. We chatted about Jorge while we waited for our meals, Smith said the previous day's surveillance revealed nothing.

It appeared my American friend felt better as he put food into his stomach but that was short-lived when we got up to leave and he made a dash for the bathroom. I felt bad for the man and covered our tab with the cash he paid me for my afternoon of surveillance. The beads of perspiration on Smith's forehead when he returned, told me he was in for a rough day.

We met Maria Cortez at a café near her church in Barra de Navidad. A pretty woman with long black hair, she was shapely and appeared to be in her early thirty's. An embroidered sun dress and shiny gold jewelry made her stand out against the tank tops and flip flops worn by strolling tourists along the main street. She sat on the patio facing the street, with her back to the coffee shop.

It was Smith's gig so I let him lead the way. He walked straight to Maria and introduced the two of us. I assumed she either told him how she looked before the meet or he simply headed for the best-looking woman in the place, hoping he'd be right. She didn't get up, but smiled and extended a hand to each of us. Perfectly manicured and painted nails graced the ends of her long and slender fingers. What could a woman like this see in a slime ball like Jorge?

Maria cut to the chase and apologized for not coming forward sooner, how we were the first investigators she agreed to speak with and she didn't trust the police. Smith thanked her for meeting with us and assured her anything we discussed would be kept confidential and only between us. Her response caught my buddy off guard, when she asked how Samantha's family was coping with her disappearance.

As a seasoned investigator Smith kept his answers short, opting to listen instead, soliciting any tidbit of information he could. Maria said she previously worked in one of the hotels in Barra but transferred to Guadalajara after the 'incident'. Before Smith could inquire, she said Jorge raped her and had gotten her pregnant.

Tears welled in her eyes and slowly rolled down her cheeks. I grabbed a wad of napkins and offered them to her. She took a moment to regain her composure. We stayed silent and let Maria tell us the story in her own words. She wiped her tears and nose, then took a deep breath and continued.

It was on her best friend's birthday when a group of women visited some of the bars in town. Their last stop was at a nightclub, the place where she met Jorge. Maria said he bought their group drinks to help the birthday girl celebrate but he wasn't her type and she paid him little attention. When she realized she'd had too much to drink, Maria said goodbye to her friends and walked a short distance to the taxi stand.

There was only one cab waiting and when she got in, Jorge was behind the wheel. He acted surprised to see her and said something to the effect of 'my lucky day'. He opened the bottle of tequila that was on the front seat and offered her a drink but she declined. Jorge pouted like a schoolchild in detention and told her the car couldn't move until she had a drink.

Against her better judgement but hoping that was all it would take to get her home, Maria complied. Jorge also took a drink, or so she thought. When he missed the first turn needed to get her home and she complained, Jorge apologized and said he'd go around the block. But then he turned further away, heading out of town.

Maria protested but suddenly felt nauseous. Assuming it was a combination of the booze she drank and the taxicab's motion, she closed her eyes and took some deep breaths. The feeling got worse and she demanded Jorge turn around and take her home. The road and neighborhood grew black around her. Darkness closed in until she couldn't see or hear anything at all.

CHAPTER FIFTY-THREE

Raped

Miss Cortez hadn't touched her iced coffee since we sat down. She cleared the second wave of tears from her face with a napkin, careful not to smear her makeup. We sat in silence, wondering if she would be able to continue. I'd heard personal accountings of rape as a police detective but her story made me feel sorry and angry at the same time.

Maria hadn't made eye contact with us since she began relating the incident but she raised her head and peered at Smith and I in turn when she said, 'He raped me'. Her gaze expressed both the pain and anger I felt but it was no contest as to who owned it. She told us it was near dawn when she woke up naked in the back of Jorge's taxi. He was passed out in the front seat.

Feeling an unusual internal pain and seeing dried blood on the inside of one thigh, she knew exactly what happened. But Maria also knew she would never have agreed to such a thing, no matter how drunk she was. The young woman was a virgin and had planned to stay that way until marriage. She took in her unfamiliar surroundings and panicked.

Maria gathered up her clothes, trying not to wake Jorge but her panties were missing. Peeking over the seat, she saw them clutched in his hand and tucked under his chin as if he was holding his baby blanket. He stirred when she opened the back door, but only rolled over and remained asleep.

Not knowing which way to go, Maria listened...her ears searching for a clue...the sound of traffic or ocean waves...anything. A faint engine noise caught her attention and she ran in that direction. She got dressed along the way. Her heels, useless on the dirt roads and grassy fields, she carried with her.

The noise got louder as she heard something like a truck motor. Running through rows of coconut trees and banana plants, she heard the ocean in the distance. A tractor appeared, a farmer working his plantation. He had a cell phone and let her use it to call her older brother. She dared not tell her parents anything yet.

Maria paused and took a long drink from her iced coffee. Smith had been squirming in his seat and finally excused himself. I felt his pain and knew what was coming for him. He scrambled away, placing each step carefully. Her eyes focused on the table directly in front of her, I sat quietly and let her regain her composure.

She started to shake and I feared a major outburst or even a breakdown so I tried to reassure her, saying it wasn't her fault and how I knew women in a similar situation. One was a niece who confided in me but I didn't go into details other than to say she'd been drugged, as the case seemed to be with Maria. She managed to hold back another wave of tears.

Smith returned to the table not looking any better than when he left. He glanced at me to see if he missed anything and I moved my head slightly to say no. Taking over the conversation, the American told Maria how sorry he was and if he had any say in the matter, Jorge would pay for what he did to her. Smith asked if she notified the authorities.

The young woman's gaze fixed on her inquisitor. Her tone grew sharp. She said that only her brother and best friend knew at the time, the same friend who had the birthday party and was an acquaintance of Jorge's sister. Maria's brother wanted to kill the man but he learned of the cab drivers cartel connections and changed his mind. Her best friend voiced the same concerns and actually suggested Maria might have led him on. She hadn't spoken to her since.

She said it was only a matter of time before her parents figured out something was wrong. Her condition sealed her fate and their religious beliefs stopped her from ending the pregnancy. Maria's mother said it was a child of God. Her father wasn't so forgiving, saying the baby was more the incarnation of Satan himself.

Smith waited for the horror story to end before he asked Maria about Samantha. She said they'd been friends when she lived in town but only heard about her going missing on the news. Moving to Guadalajara kept her away from Jorge and she only returned to Barra for a family christening at the church. In closing, Maria said she loved her daughter and Jorge would never know about her. He would eventually have to answer to God for his sins.

We thanked Maria for her time and wished her well. After Smith paid the check, she said she could draw us a map of where Jorge took her. He asked how she remembered and Maria said her brother made her show him where she found the farmer. They figured it out from there. Smith pulled out a pen and tore a page from his notebook and slid them across the table. He turned to me with a look of satisfaction. Then I heard his stomach roar.

CHAPTER FIFTY-FOUR

The Return

I was overdue for a visit to the beach table and admittedly curious to see if anyone else in the murder club had anything new to report. Everyone was cheerful and chatty and talking about everything else but the missing and murdered when I got there. Even Bruce seemed better, engaged in a conversation with Big Willy about the latest book he was reading.

Barely into my seat, Sticks asked about my friend, John Smith. Wanda and Katie giggled like school girls who had been talking about the captain of the football team. "I hear he's pretty buff, with a washboard stomach I could rub my...um, clothes on. Sorry, I missed meeting him, Ed."

The women laughed out loud. I turned to Willy who'd puffed his chest out and did his best at a Popeye pose to show off his biceps. "He's busy following up on information we got from one of Jorge's victims yesterday. But Willy and I can peel off our shirts and put on a show for you."

Wanda rubbed Willy's belly and gave him a big squeeze. "I love you just the way you are, honey."

I grabbed a beer from our cooler and popped the top. Wanda asked, "What do you mean, one of Jorge's victims...you mean a witness to someone he killed?"

Letting cold beer slip down my throat before answering, I filled the group in on our chat with Maria and what happened to her. Tequila Tommy appeared right when I mentioned the word rape. "We've got rapes now...to go with the murders?"

I held a hand up to stop him and continued with my story and how Smith was going to check out the crime scene, according to Maria's map. Tommy said it sounded like the area where he went on an ATV tour. There was nothing but miles of coconut and banana groves. I finished my story with the pregnancy just as Trudi and Rudi stopped by.

Normally, she'd start by telling us what everyone was up to, including the latest gossip, but instead she asked who was pregnant. Knowing the shortest answer is always the best one, I simply told her it was our maid's daughter. Trombone Trudi was something I liked to call her. She was always blowing her horn but didn't know our maid only had a son.

I'd learned to avoid the duo when seeing them on my morning walks, always making sure I was on the opposite side of the street, avoiding eye contact. Any acknowledgement of their presence meant at least twenty minutes getting the latest news. Rudi played on the beach with his dog, as usual. It wasn't until he wandered off, that Trudi said a quick goodbye and decided to follow her husband.

Before any further conversation, Bruce grunted loudly. He had one eye closed to avoid the smoke that drifted up from a cigarette tucked in one corner of his mouth. His book in one hand, he excitedly pointed down the beach with the other. Morty, who had been sitting quietly nursing a bad hangover, said, "Forgot to tell you folks...Chief Alvarez said they had no case against Amigo and finally had to release him."

Bruce jumped up from his seat and ran off to greet his long-lost twin.

CHAPTER FIFTY-FIVE

The Coconut Grove

John Smith did his best to follow Maria's hand-drawn map to where she believed Jorge assaulted her. There were several dirt roads running off the main highway, into groves of coconut and banana trees. He turned onto the one where the rusted remains of an old truck marked the entrance. It headed southeast towards the ocean, which was nowhere in sight.

The American PI took a fork in the road, edged by fencing along one piece of property. He'd never seen so many banana trees and wondered about the blue bags that covered the fruit. Everything was so green and lush. Tall coconut trees grew amongst the bananas. Smith came to a sandy clearing where there was an old irrigation shack with pipes running off in different directions into the fields.

Maria's map showed a similar structure but didn't say what it was. Smith parked and got out of the car to look around. Tire tracks led to and from the building but appeared to have been made by a tractor. The shack's door was padlocked, with no windows to see anything inside. He walked the perimeter and stopped out front, where there were discarded cigarette butts on the ground.

Smith considered the tracks and butts and decided to bag a couple of them in the hopes one of his sources would be able to check them for DNA. He'd already collected samples from discarded items Jorge left behind while under surveillance. Walking the fence line and back up the road a way, he couldn't find any tire tracks that might have been made by a car or taxicab.

Heading back to his rental, Smith shook his head and thought it was a waste of time. He'd hoped there might be fresh evidence of Jorge being there but the rape was so long ago that any sign of him would be long gone. The private eye got back into his car and checked the map one more time for good measure. He decided it was hopeless.

Smith started the car and put it in gear. He had to make a three-point turn to get back to the highway but in doing so buried the front drive wheels in loose sand. He got out to have a look and then tried to rock the car back and forth, shifting from drive to reverse. It was no use, he was stuck.

CHAPTER FIFTY-SIX

A Clue

Irritated by a ringing cell phone and wondering who brought theirs with them, I scanned our gang at the table to find the culprit. But they were looking at me and the noise that came from my cooler bag. Shit. I forgot I started carrying it after connecting with John Smith.

Retrieving the device from the side pocket, I answered the call. Everyone else I knew was at the table so Smith had to be the caller. My new friend said he was stuck in the sand on the dirt road where Maria said she was attacked. Asking if I could come to his rescue, I said I wasn't about to get my Impala stuck trying to pull him out. Thinking for a moment about another solution, I told him to stay put while I tried to find help.

He thanked me saying he wasn't going anywhere and the walk back to the highway would probably kill him. He'd be waiting under a shady palm tree. I glanced over at Willy, his tank top already sweat-soaked. "Ya wanna go for a ride and cool down, big guy?"

I was offered one of his signature expressions, a scrunched nose and pursed lips. "Are we gonna ride around in the Impala with the AC on? Should I bring beer?"

I chuckled. "No, buddy, I gotta go find Fred and see if we can use the Flintstone buggy for a tow job...John Smith's got himself stuck in the sand, down the highway."

Willy glanced at Wanda for permission. She waived him off. "Sure, let's go rescue the dumb gumshoe...doesn't he know you need a 4-wheeler for driving on sand?" He smiled. "Unless it's the Impala with Edmundo behind the wheel."

We walked back up to the apartments and I saw Fred's dune buggy in his parking spot. It took forever for him to answer the door. By his groggy and disheveled appearance, he didn't need to tell us he'd been sleeping. "Bit early for a nap, ain't it, Fred?"

"Why, what time is it...does it really matter? I'm retired and was tired and got fuck-all else to do."

"John Smith went and got himself stuck in one of the farm fields down the highway...I was thinking you might help us winch him out with your buggy."

He nodded. "Why don't I just give you the keys and go back to bed?"

I glanced at Willy and considered his offer. "I've never driven anything like that and don't want to break it...never used a winch before."

Fred used the back of his hand to wipe the sleep from his eyes and pushed the door open further. "C'mon in out of the sun...I'll put some clothes on." He stumbled around the kitchen as if looking for something.

"Did you lose your keys?"

"My phone. I'm gonna call Victor...he's got an ATV and knows all those farm roads. We'd get lost out there...all the damn trees look the same."

As luck would have it, Victor was just about to head out for some groceries and said he'd stop by and lead the way out to the coconut groves. I jumped in with him, while Willy rode with Fred.

My chauffeur asked if I knew exactly where Smith was so I tried to explain what I recalled from Maria's map.

I thought we were looking for a rusted-out car but it was an old truck that marked the farm road into the coconut and banana groves. Fred and Willy followed Victor and I on the dirt track to a fork, where I pointed out the way to go. We drove for at least another half-mile until the road dead-ended near an old shack. There was no car or John Smith anywhere in sight.

Victor shut off the engine and I climbed out to see if Smith was stuck off the road, somewhere out of sight. The others did the same but the American was nowhere to be found. We all gathered in front of the shack, dumfounded.

"I'm sorry, Vic, this is where he said he was...at a dead end, near the shack."

He smiled. "Your friend will be somewhere in these fields... near another shack is my guess. They're pump houses, put up about every kilometer or so for irrigation. He'll be on a parallel road out here, somewhere. Can you call him and ask which way he came in?"

I did and Smith answered on the first ring.

"We're here...where are you?"

"Right here where I said, where are you?"

"Tell me your route in from the highway."

"I followed the map." I heard the sound of rustling paper as he double-checked. "I turned off at the rusty truck and took the fork in the road where the fence starts...all the way to the shack."

I laughed, but not too hard. "I just learned those shacks are scattered all over the farm...they're pump-houses for irrigation. One of us is on the wrong road."

Smith didn't laugh. "For fuck's sake...it doesn't matter much at this point. Can you go back to the fork and turn the other way at the fence...that should get you to me."

"See ya soon...I hope."

The guys mounted back up but I stepped to the side of the road to take a leak. After I finished and turned back to the ATV, I noticed something shiny in the sand. I scooped up a woman's earing, checked it out, and stuffed it in my pocket. We drove back up the road, made a turn at the fork, and finally found Smith. He looked relieved but exhausted.

"Thank God you guys found me, I was about to start calling towing companies but had no idea how to tell them where I was."

Fred and Victor went to work rigging up the winch to Smith's rental car. Willy handed him a cold beer.

Smith grinned. "Where'd you get that?"

Willy scoffed. "It's like they say in that credit card commercial. 'I never leave home without it'."

After Smith downed half his beer, I pulled out the earing and showed it to him. "Where'd you get that?"

"On the other dead-end road with a pump house...mean anything to you?"

He took it, held it up to the sun and examined it more closely. "I got nothing...you?"

"You have those photos of Samantha Adams with you?"

"Yeah...my briefcase, in the car. Why?"

"Grab 'em, will ya?"

Smith stepped over the winch cable while the guys reeled in the slack. He returned with a folder, flipped it open and thumbed through the photographs he'd been given by the family. My friend pulled out one image and placed it on top the closed folder. "Let me see that earing again, Ed." He compared it to a set Adams was wearing in the picture. "Holy fuck!"

CHAPTER FIFTY-SEVEN

Now What?

On Victor's advice, we left the coconut grove and regrouped back at the Fenix Resort where we called a hasty meeting of the murder club. In his opinion there wasn't enough daylight left to do any kind of a serious search of the grove and his ATV didn't have proper lights for driving at night. Fred agreed since he never took his rig anywhere after dark.

John Smith wasn't happy, wanting to go back to the area where I found the earing in hopes of finding more evidence that might help him discover what happened to Samantha Adams. He reported back to her father daily and was tired of having nothing new to tell the distraught man. Being the logical sort, he agreed waiting another day wasn't going to mean much in the overall scope of his investigation.

Katie texted the other women and spread the word to gather the rest of the group at our place. She suggested everyone bring something to eat and we'd have a potluck barbeque while we conducted our meeting. Instead of a shower, I decided a swim was in order to clean up and cool off at the same time. Willy agreed, saying why waste good soap when you have a pool full of chlorine. Wanda had returned to their apartment after the beach so he called and told her to bring beer when she came for dinner.

Fred disappeared and we assumed he went back upstairs to finish his nap.

Willy said it was nearly impossible to communicate with him in the buggy, over the engine noise and having to get close enough to his bad ear to kiss him.

Smith was happy to be rescued and offered to pay Victor for his trouble. He refused to take any money but accepted an invitation to join us for dinner at the resort. The PI said he'd supply the tequila. I made sure to text Morty, figuring he'd be keen on hearing the latest in our ongoing investigation.

As our gang gathered under the pergola, separate conversations broke out. The guys talked about the four-wheel and winch action earlier in the day. The women fretted over what John Smith would be wearing when he got there. There wasn't a peep from any of them when he walked in the gate carrying a box of beer and bottle of top shelf tequila.

He'd cleaned up since we pulled his car out of the sand. His short black wavy hair was gelled into perfect position and he was clean shaven. The blue and white Hawaiian shirt over crisp white shorts made his steel-blue eyes pop. The ladies tripped over each other trying to usher him in. Hell, if I was a woman, I would do him.

Tommy was the last to arrive and he was introduced to Smith for the first time. "I hear you've been busy, trying to track down that Adams woman."

The American PI took his cue from Tommy's remark and ran with it, bringing everyone up to date about his investigation. He explained how his work was usually confidential but he felt our little club had been helpful and therefore trustworthy, in his opinion. Smith took us all by surprise when he said that Samantha's father was now offering a one-hundred-thousand-dollar reward for information leading to the discovery of his daughter's whereabouts.

He went on to say that Mrs. Adams still believed Samantha was alive but her father was more of a realist and assumed the money would be paid upon the discovery of her body. The mention of a reward spurred whispers around the table and GP said, "That's like 140k in Canuck dollars."

A few dirty looks from the women landed on him.

"What? That's a lot of money...the man obviously wants his daughter found, dead or alive."

Helen spoke up. "That's a bit harsh, don't you think, honey?"

"I'm just being honest." He glanced around the table. "You can't tell me nobody else around this table isn't thinking about the money."

Katie threw her two cents in. "I agree with the mayor, that's kind of morbid talking like that...like she's dead already." She turned to Smith. "Do you think there's any chance she's still alive, John?"

Silence filled the air. He frowned. "In my experience with this sort of thing...no, I think she's dead and buried...maybe somewhere in the coconut groves where we were today. It's a perfect spot to hide a body. And I can't prove it yet, but my gut tells me Jorge is the man who killed her. He's the last person she was seen with and has a history of abusing women."

Wanda asked, "But weren't they dating...why would he kill her if that's the case?"

Smith answered. "That's a good question and I don't have an answer for you." He looked around the table. "But I'm hoping to get more answers tomorrow and that some of you will come back to the groves with me to have another look and maybe dig around."

Wilma jumped in. "Fred and I are in...Victor, don't you have a metal detector? Maybe bring that and some shovels."

Fred looked puzzled and turned to his wife. "Honey, that's not very nice calling Victor mental because he lives in a hovel."

We ignored Fred, while others chimed in and volunteered to help with the search. While the excursion was being organized by the men, the women started prepping food for dinner. As usual, GP took the opportunity to set up a line of tequila shots, poured from Smith's expensive bottle. He called out, "Grab a glass everyone, and let's toast to digging for dollars."

CHAPTER FIFTY-EIGHT

Sand Box

Tequila did the talking the previous night, when all the men and a few of the women said they planned to go along for the treasure hunt. When we saddled up in the morning it was those who shied away from the cactus juice that showed up. The plan was to meet at the Costalegre Tour Company, where Smith had rented four-wheelers for those of us who didn't want to repeat his mistake.

Like the day before, Willy and I rode over there with Fred and Victor. GP, Helen and Katie took their bicycles. My wife said she'd rather not ride with Fred in the dune buggy, after our experience of rolling one of the ATV rentals our first year in Melaque. I broke two ribs in the mishap and she got pretty banged up.

After everyone had their ass in a seat, Victor led the way out to the coconut groves. To avoid the highway, he took us down the beach and along dirt paths and farm roads. It was a bumpy twenty-minute ride but we had a chance to enjoy different scenery in the early morning light. The air was cool at that time of day and felt great.

Our tour guide stopped near the pump shack where I found the earring. All that jostling around irritated a few bladders, including mine and Katie's. When she asked where she could pee, Victor said, "women behind the shack, men pick a tree."

John Smith asked me where I found the earing and I really wasn't sure until I saw our tire tracks from the day before. He asked everyone to fan out across the dirt road, standing an arm's length apart, and then to slowly move away from the shack. "Like you see in the movies when they do a grid search."

Victor had his metal detector and asked if it would help. Smith said it couldn't hurt and told him to fall in behind us and perhaps find something we might miss. We did as he asked and slowly moved along, searching the ground in front of us. Some stooped to pick up little shiny things, finding pieces of broken glass.

Helen pointed to a cigarette butt and asked if they could get DNA from it, like they do on CSI. Smith told her not to touch it and he scooped it into a small envelope. "You never know, Helen, sometimes it pans out...I have samples of Jorge's DNA so we might be able to prove he was here if this butt is good enough to test."

Soon, Smith had a pocket full of discarded butt samples. Obviously, someone liked to smoke in that particular spot on the dead-end road. Victor's machine beeped more often than not, detecting small pieces of metal, wire, beer caps and a ten-centavo coin. There were also soiled tissues and a used condom that nobody dared touch. Smith cursed but bagged it.

After about a hundred yards and diminishing debris, Smith had us turn around and double back for good measure. The round trip took us almost an hour. The sun had risen to a position where it beat down on us, leaving Willy and I with sweat-stained shirts. The group retreated to the shade of a palm tree for a break. Fred took a nap.

Like a kid with his new toy, Victor continued working his metal detector around the area. Being a fulltime expat, he'd acclimatized to the subtropical temperatures and humidity. Something that I was never lucky enough to experience, no matter where I travelled to.

A high-pitched screech from his machine caught our attention. He was behind the pump shack, near some overgrown shrubs. Victor waived the device back and forth and every time he got near the bush it screeched.

We all assumed it was just another piece of junk metal but Smith went to investigate. Victor kicked some of the growth aside, reached down and came up with a shovel in his hand. Normally, that tool wouldn't warrant a second thought in a plot of farmland. But it was a foldable military-type shovel, the kind you'd take backpacking or camping.

John glanced at me, wondering if I was thinking the same thing. I was, and walked over to join him. "I know it's a farm and all, but wouldn't you think they'd keep their tools in the shed...and would use a larger shovel?"

I nodded. "Yeah...I guess. Let me have a closer look at it." Victor handed me the shovel. It was a bit dirty and weathered from laying in the bushes but a lack of rust and sharp edge made me believe it wasn't that old. "Okay, I agree...it shouldn't be here but..."

Smith had already moved on, kicking around loose parts of the shrubbery. "Victor, run that thing over the ground around here. Some of this stuff is like tumbleweed that's not anchored in the soil."

He followed the private investigator, stabbing his device into small open patches where it wouldn't get tangled in the weeds. Smith kept getting his feet stuck in the thicket but then found an opening where nothing was rooted. "Check around here, Vic."

When his machine screamed it had detected metal, Smith looked back over his shoulder at me. I thought he had a gut feeling but it didn't make any sense and I asked, "I know you're hoping she might be buried out here, but a metal detector won't tell you that."

He shook his head. "There's where you'd be wrong my friend...Samantha has titanium in her left leg...something she got after being hit by a car. Her father said she was always setting off metal detectors in airports."

I heard rustling of footsteps; the rest of the gang gathered around me. I handed Smith the shovel. "The honor is all yours, buddy, happy digging."

Willy spoke up. "We could be here all day, trying to dig six feet down with that little shovel."

GP scoffed. "Have you ever tried to dig a hole on the beach or in the sand, big guy? Look what we're standing on. There's no way you could dig a full grave here with a simple shovel...the loose sand would keep filling in the hole."

Smith told GP he was right and he'd experienced that in what they called 'the sandbox' during his tours in the Middle East. It was the reason they used sandbags. He'd only removed a few shovelfuls of sand when he stopped and bent over. It was a piece of metal wire. "Great, more garbage...probably all kinds of it around this pump shack. Old pipes and other crap. "He yanked hard to pull the wire from the ground. It was wrapped around and attached to something bigger.

"Holy shit!"

CHAPTER FIFTY-NINE

Buried

The women gasped and stepped back. Curious, GP and Willy stood their ground. Like any seasoned cop, I moved in for a closer look. Smith had pulled up a pair of legs with wire wrapped around the ankles. They appeared to belong to a woman and the extremities didn't show heavy signs of decomposition. He handed me the shovel and we gingerly extricated more of the body from its sandy grave.

Helen called out. "Isn't this where we call the police?"

John Smith snapped back. "I gotta see if it's her first." He checked the lower left leg for a surgery scar but the skin was discolored, making it difficult to tell.

I commented. "I've read that the dry sand slows decomp...like with Egyptian mummies found in the desert. It'll be hard to tell how long she's been here unless..."

Smith was a step ahead of me. He worked the torso and then head free. "It's not her...hair color is wrong. Fuck. Now we need to call the police. Better yet...Ed, do you have a way to contact Chief Alvarez?"

I didn't have a number for the chief and had to call Morty. He took forever to answer the phone and said he had to go back to bed because of his lingering hangover. I told him we discovered a body and he literally dropped the phone. I heard him fumbling to retrieve it and he cleared the frog from his throat. "Holy shit...you really found the Adams woman?"

"No, buddy, we found a different woman. We need you to call Alvarez so he can send his people out."

"I can't believe it. How...where'd you find her?"

"The coconut grove...like we talked about last night."

He coughed for about ten seconds. "Wow...crazy, I'll call him right away. You need anything else?"

"We're good, gracias, Amigo." In detective mode, I'd forgotten about the others. They were gathered under the shade tree. Katie was watching me, she looked like she was about to lose her breakfast. Helen was crying. GP did his best to console her. Willy had cracked a beer and was sitting against the tree, looking a bit shell-shocked. Fred was still fast asleep.

Smith was down on one knee, examining the body. "I'm no medical examiner, Ed, there's not much I can tell except she was well-dressed, as if she was out for the night. Her dress is torn on one shoulder...could have been raped or in a fight...who knows?" He glanced at Victor, who was sitting by himself, up against the pump shack. "You think we should look some more before the cops get here?"

I thought about it for a moment. Shrugged. "Guess it can't hurt...better us getting the reward than crooked cops."

Smith shook his head. "Ooh...you're cold, man. But hey, my client won't care who the money goes to. He just wants his daughter found."

We put Victor back to work, searching a grid pattern around the grave site we discovered. The rest of the gang stayed in the shade; they'd had enough fun for one day. I told them they could head back home if they wanted but Willy waived me off and said they'd stick around a bit longer. Victor moved his magic wand around for another twenty minutes, only hitting on more metal junk. Then a brand-new pickup truck came down the dirt road, heading in our direction. It wasn't the police.

A middle-aged Mexican man got out and started waving and yelling at us. Having no idea what he was saying, I could only assume he was telling us to get off his land. When he got close to the grave site he froze in his tracks. Victor spoke Spanish well enough that he was able to explain to the man what was going on.

He was not happy and said we should get out of there before he called the police. Victor told him they were already on the way and we intended to stick around. The farmer said the cops would not be pleased seeing gringos digging up dead bodies. Then, perhaps in an attempt to appease the man, Victor told him there was a cash reward involved.

The farmer gave us all a good look and stood there, scratching his head. That's when we heard the sirens; the police were on the way. Two cars, by what we could see. I recognized the chief's Suburban, followed by a marked car. I leaned in closer to Victor. "Did I hear you tell him about the reward?"

"Yeah, the way things work for us gringos in Mexico, we could find ourselves arrested for murder."

"Did you tell him it was a hundred K?"

"No, I said ten."

"Dollars or pesos?"

Victor smiled. "I didn't specify."

CHAPTER SIXTY

The Dog

Chief Alvarez recognized me and nodded but before he could get too close the farmer cut him off and gave him an earful. The two uniformed officers stood behind him awaiting further instructions. Once again, I couldn't understand any of the rapid-fire conversation in Spanish. Victor tried to interpret parts he overheard and said the farmer was carrying on about reward money and getting the dead woman off his property.

The police chief finally pushed the farmer aside and stepped up to the freshly opened gravesite. Before the farmer verbally attacked him again, I introduced John Smith and told the top cop who he was and why he was there. Alvarez took in my friend. "Americano, hey...and some rich countryman of yours is paying a reward for the discovery of this woman?"

I kept my mouth shut. It seemed everyone wanted a piece of the pie for themselves and it was no surprise to me the police would include themselves. Smith stopped the chief short of claiming his prize when he emphasized the body at our feet was not the woman we were searching for. Alvarez must have missed that part, gone deaf after the mention of reward money.

Smith quickly reminded the chief that it was Samantha Adams he was hired to find and Jorge was his number one suspect after receiving information from a previous rape victim. She was the one who led us to the place where we were standing, the site of her sexual assault. Some of the color drained from Alvarez's face. "Mama Mia...not him again."

The farmer tried to step in between Smith and the chief but he was a little guy and I placed my hulking frame in front of him. Trying to get around me would have put him in the grave so he tried calling out to the chief. Alvarez shouted something to the annoying man and kept him at bay.

Smith went on to tell him we found one of Samantha's earrings about two hundred feet from where we were standing and we had discarded cigarette butts that would put Jorje at the scene, but we needed her body to make the case. It was like the chief was struck by a lightning bolt that jump-started his brain. He pulled out his phone, made a call, then ordered the uniformed cops to guard the body.

Smith, Victor and I joined the others who still huddled in the shade, watching the show. We filled in the peanut gallery as to what was going on, as far as we knew. Victor mentioned how the farmer and now the police, wanted to claim the reward for themselves. Smith chuckled. "Mr. Adams has left that up to me so we'll see who gets what."

Victor said, "I heard the chief ask someone to bring a cadaver dog and to find someone with a backhoe. The farmer said he had one and the two of them argued over who would be covering the operator's cost."

I asked Smith, "You told Alvarez the cigarette butts belonged to Jorge...bit of a stretch, don't you think?"

He smiled. "Whatever it takes to find our girl."

Within twenty minutes, two more police cars rolled in. Three more cops and one large German shepherd. The two uniforms followed the dog-handler with shovels in hand. Rover was led to our gravesite, perhaps to remind the pooch what he was looking for. On a mission from there, it was as if he was searching for a bone he buried. Within five minutes, the dog stopped and sat at attention, indicating there was death underground.

I stayed back with the gang but Smith joined the chief to watch his men while they dug. The farmer made an attempt to join them but was strong-armed by one of the cops. It was another shallow grave and another female corpse. On their knees, the two uniforms gently brushed away the sand from the woman's head. She was lying face up.

When Smith dropped to one knee, I knew his search was over. Once again, the lack of decomposition allowed him to positively identify Samantha Adams. He caught my gaze and nodded. I turned to tell the others but teary eyes said that they already knew. Katie wrapped her arms around me and hugged me hard. Helen did the same to GP. Willy dropped his beer can and stood in silence with his mouth agape. Fred awoke from his coma. "What's with the dog?"

It was as if we'd known the victim her whole life and were gathered to say our final farewell. I knew how important it is for most families to get closure and hoped the Adams would finally find peace when they received the news. Smith didn't waste any time and stepped away from Samantha to make the call.

He was on the phone speaking to Mr. Adams when the dog handler called out. It was another body.

CHAPTER SIXTY-ONE

Aftermath

With the discovery of the third body, the gang had enough. Chief Alvarez asked John Smith to stick around but the rest of us were allowed to leave. I thought the top cop was actually smiling when we left, probably thinking there were less people to split the reward money with. It was the last thing on our minds driving home. Somehow the scenery wasn't as impressive and the ride seemed longer.

Arriving back at the Fenix resort, we went our separate ways. Willy and I jumped in the pool to cool off, others said they needed a shower to wash away the stench of death. When I went inside, Katie was crying and told me her clothes still smelled. As a cop and having dealt with all sorts of bodies in different states of decomposition, I knew the pungent odor too well. I gave my wife a big hug.

Katie said she wasn't in the mood to cook and didn't feel like socializing with anyone else at the resort. After we were both dressed, I suggested we walk down to the El Dorado and watch the pelicans diving for their dinner. They made a decent margarita there and she looked like she could use a couple. I ordered the same. We ignored our menus and stared at the panorama in front of us.

The sun performed its magic, a lemon becoming an orange, the sky changing from shades of blue into indigo and burgundy. Spindly clouds closed in like curtains, signaling the end of another show. The server waited patiently behind the bar, having been waived off after delivering our drinks. Our lingering moment of tranquility was interrupted by my phone, I'd forgotten about it in Katie's purse.

It was John Smith, my reminder of reality and the cruel world we live in. He said there were six bodies in total, all women. His last word made me wonder who was killing the men and what had happened to our little beach town. John said he was done for the day and wondered if we could hook up for dinner. He understood when I told him we didn't have much of an appetite.

Returning home, I saw GP sitting on his balcony with a glass of scotch in one hand and a cigar in the other. There was none of the usual music in the background and he never said a peep. He just stared off into the night sky. Their apartment was in darkness and I assumed Helen had gone to bed. Fred and Wilma's apartment was dark and quiet too. The events of that day completely sucked all the joy out of our happy resort.

A New Day

I popped a hard-boiled egg in my mouth before my morning walk. We barely ate anything the night before and I needed the energy boost. Searching my mind for more pleasant topics to think about, I tried to plan the next book chapter in my head. On second thought, the story was all about murder and I needed a break from that.

Changing the channel to travel, I thought about our summer destination. We'd planned a trip to Croatia, starting in Budapest, Hungary, then working our way down through Slovenia and Croatia to the Adriatic coast. We'd be on a train, in a rental car and on a small cruise ship, going as far south as Mostar in Bosnia. I had the whole itinerary laid out like a CAA trip ticket, with only a few small details to iron out before we went.

Walking by the bank, I saw Tommy exiting the parking lot on his motorcycle. He spotted me and pulled up to the curb. "I heard you guys had quite the day, yesterday. Glad I was hungover...I didn't need to see that. Probably no big deal for you, eh, Ed?"

I flipped my eyebrows and dabbed sweat from my forehead. "Can't say it bothers me too much, but it's still not something I like to see. I don't miss that part of the job. It was especially sad seeing and knowing what happened to those women."

"Do you think Jorge killed them?"

"Probably, but that has yet to be proven. John Smith is still working on it with the cops...for what that's worth. They seemed more concerned with getting their hands on the reward money."

Tommy fastened the chin strap on his helmet and reached for the ignition switch, preparing to leave. Then he lowered his sunglasses and smiled. "Did you hear about Gary?"

"No. Shit, did they find his body too?"

He shook his head from side to side. "Nope. Just walked into the her house, kissed Allison and told her he was hungry."

"What?!"

"Yup. She said he was still wearing the same clothes he had on when he went golfing, minus his shoes. And he remembers looking for his ball behind the twelfth green but nothing else until he woke up near Twiggs bar. Allison said he looks no worse for the wear except for a sun blister on his neck."

Tommy flipped up his kickstand and fired up the engine. "I'm really sorry about the women but glad my buddy's home safe and sound." He feigned a salute and rode off. I stood there for almost another full minute, flabbergasted. Then I wondered about the 'sun blister' and if it was the same mark that Bruce and Amigo had. That shit was getting weird.

Having lost my rhythm, I decided to pop my head into the spot where Morty and I sometimes met for breakfast. He was there and hadn't eaten yet so I placed my order with the waiter on the way to his table. The big man gave me a once-over. "Reliving your detective days, are ya?"

"You heard?"

"Small town. Everyone has. Plus, there was a clip on the news last night—we get it with English subtitles. The cops wouldn't let media anywhere near the dump site, but they got footage of them hauling bodies away." He lifted his cup and took a sip of coffee. "My buddy, the chief, declined to comment, saying the matter was still under investigation...how many times you use that line?"

I clucked. "More than a few. I was always amazed when they caught me pulling up to a crime scene and wanted a comment on something that hadn't even been investigated yet. They're like vultures waiting for fresh roadkill."

"One of the victims was the Adams woman?"

"Yeah, Smith confirmed it. He had to call her father...bet that went over like a fart in church."

Morty had his top lip in the coffee, sipping, and almost spewed. "Christ, Ed, I do miss the old days sometimes...the cop humor. That and booze, hey? Our coping mechanisms...not like all the psycho-babble shit they have available these days. We turned out okay, didn't we?"

I laughed. "Depends who you ask. My wife never knew me as a cop...maybe why she fell in love with me. But I hear ya, times have changed and they couldn't pay me enough to do it all over again."

Our breakfasts arrived and silence fell over the table as we got down to business.

CHAPTER SIXTY-THREE

The Payoff

That day was a quiet one. Katie couldn't believe my news about Gary, when I returned home after breakfast and told her of his homecoming. She was happy for Allison and said it was nice to hear some good news for a change. I didn't bother to tell her about the mark on his neck. She took her bike out for a ride and planned to pick up a few groceries while she was out. I got my laptop and sat on the patio, hoping to knock off a chapter or two.

Everyone in the resort seemed to be avoiding each other or keeping to themselves. I saw Wilma in the pool for a bit, with Fred relaxing in the sun, but that was the only action in the courtyard all day. Even John Smith kept his distance. I was sure he realized that besides me and Morty, nobody else was quite used to seeing the ugly side of humanity.

He called after dinner, asking how everyone was doing. I was honest and told him I thought the murder club had run its course. When I mentioned our friend Gary returning home, he found the timing interesting and said it was kind of like the theory about one person being born when another dies. I countered that we were owed five more births.

John told me he had a long conversation with his employer, Mr. Adams, who wanted justice for his daughter. The man said there would be no closure for him until Jorge or whomever was responsible for her death was held accountable. In a roundabout way, the wealthy American even suggested he wouldn't be terribly upset if the suspected killer fell victim to some sort of 'accident'.

I could tell the suggestion upset Smith. He told me he'd done some stupid and terrible things when his government paid him to fight for his country, but he was no mercenary or contract killer. They also discussed the reward and whom it should be paid to since no one in particular, other than our team effort, was solely responsible for finding Samantha.

One could argue semantics, saying Maria led us to the crime scene and I found the earring or Victor discovered the first body, but I left it alone. I don't think anyone thought anymore about the money after what we saw in that coconut grove. But Smith said money wasn't important to the grieving father and he told the PI to do 'whatever it takes' to find the man who killed his daughter.

That led him back to Police Chief Alvarez. When Smith pushed him to expedite potential DNA evidence from the crime scene and to put men on Jorge, their number one suspect, the top cop said those things were expensive and cost money. He said his police budget didn't allow for such extravagances and that maybe Smith's rich American friends might be willing to help.

It was obvious the chief was still interested in getting paid more for his services than his salary allowed. If he couldn't get a piece of the reward pie, he wasn't shy about being creative to find another way to build his retirement fund. Smith expected and was prepared for the greedy request, having gotten prior approval from his client.

He said he planned to put a tracker on Jorge's taxi ASAP and take up surveillance on him again. That's when he asked if I was still interested in helping out. Hesitating, I told him to let me sleep on it.

In all honesty, I was worried about getting involved in doing 'whatever it took', and the possible fallout from Jorge's cartel connections. After all, Melaque was my winter home and I didn't want to be continually looking over my shoulder while I was there.

Smith's plan was to pay the chief half the reward up front to get him off his ass, and the other half if and when he was able to build a case against Jorge and actually arrest him. He said he wasn't sure if the chief would come through, especially with the suspect's powerful connections, but it wasn't his money that would be lost.

He was to meet the chief in the morning, going over the details and donating to the chief's retirement fund, which included a fishing boat. "Mexican corruption at its best", John said, "Almost as bad as American politics."

My reluctance to get involved was understandable, he added, but he hoped we could stay in touch either way. I assured him I'd give him an answer the next day.

CHAPTER SIXTY-FOUR

Predictable

John Smith had barely gotten the tracking device installed on the taxi, when Jorge's phone woke him from an afternoon nap on his favorite bench. Earlier in the day, the PI took advantage of a distraction in the square, where two stray dogs were having sex and got stuck together. With everyone watching the canine porno show, he was able to duck behind the car and attach the tracker.

Jorge took the call and headed away from downtown, into the barrio on the other side of the highway. Smith had followed his target into that area before, where dead-end roads made it difficult for surveillance. That's where the tracking device came in handy, he could sit several blocks away and follow the cab's movements on his cell phone.

He positioned himself so that Jorge would have to drive by him when he retreated from the barrio. Five minutes later he did exactly that, having picked up a female passenger. Smith only got a quick glimpse when they passed by. It was a young dark-haired woman that appeared to be a local, and she sat in the front seat. He drove west and stopped at a nail salon in Villa Obregon.

The American got a better look at the woman when she exited the cab. She was attractive and dressed well, in her mid-thirties. He thought it strange when Jorge remained at the curb out front. Slouched in the driver's seat, it appeared he was trying to finish his nap. Smith was parked far enough away he was able to step out and grab a couple tacos from a roadside stand nearby.

After an hour, exactly, the woman came out of the salon and got back into the front passenger side of the cab. Jorge's head popped back into view and he drove on. They headed toward the main square next and stopped at a bakery. His female passenger got out at the curb and returned with what appeared to be a cake.

Smith wondered to himself how well Jorge knew his fare. Since she sat up front with him, was he simply helping a friend run her errands or did the two of them have some other type of relationship? She did seem to be his type. Smith considered the different women he'd seen in their shallow graves, in different stages of decomposition. It was difficult to be sure but they appeared to be similar in age and body type.

Other than Samantha Adams, none of the other women were identified at the scene, and the way the Mexican authorities worked, Smith doubted it would happen any time soon. Like the good old police chief pointed out, things like DNA testing were very expensive and put a strain on his budget. Who was going to speak on behalf of the dead women or offer closure to their families?

Would the Chief or any local authorities step up and actually make a case against Jorge? Smith highly doubted it and hoped the man did something stupid so he could respond accordingly and put an end to the madness. The taxi headed towards Barra de Navidad and he followed from a safe distance. It would have been nice to have his buddy, Ed, help out but Smith understood his reasons for staying out of it.

Instead of a four or five-man team, the tracking device made single man surveillance possible. The taxi weaved its way through downtown Barra, veering left and staying on the road running parallel to the harbor. Jorge tucked his cab into a parking spot and the two of them went up the stairs to a place called Bill's Treehouse. The woman appeared to be more than just a fare.

Smith sat around the corner, with an eye on the restaurant. True to its name, the business was somewhat built into a giant tree that appeared as old as the town itself. Its canopy shaded the whole neighborhood. They sat by the railing, across the table from each other. Considering their body language, Smith was convinced they were more than just casual acquaintances.

Dusk fell upon the Costalegre and the big tree came to life with hundreds of twinkle lights. *How romantic*, Smith thought, and he only hoped the woman wasn't Jorge's next victim. If that was his plan the American would be all over him.

Call it revenge or payback for Samantha or justice for all the women the asshole abused or murdered. There was no doubt in his mind that the handsome cab driver was a sadistic serial killer.

They had a couple drinks at Bill's, then got back into the cab and drove over to the ocean side of town and parked near the Paradise Night Club. The woman carried the cake with her when they went inside. Smith noticed pink and white Happy Birthday balloons tied up near the front door. It appeared quiet at first but soon other groups of women and some couples showed up.

Smith thought it would be nice to see what was going on inside the club but he knew Jorge wouldn't do anything there with so many other people aground. If he was predictable at all, the PI would have to wait and see what the target did with the woman when he left the bar. Knowing he'd be waiting for a while; Smith went across the street to a café and got himself a large coffee and homemade tart.

CHAPTER SIXTY-FIVE

Flying Solo

Dusk became darkness and Barra's streets grew quiet as strolling tourists finished dinner and headed home for the night. What should have been silence as most folks crawled into bed, was interrupted by thumping base from the loud music inside the Paradise Club where the birthday part was taking place. From almost a block away, it felt to Smith like his heart was pounding in his ears.

He breathed a sigh of relief when people finally started leaving the night club. Their loud and boisterous voices echoed off the stucco buildings along the street. Some walked away and disappeared around the corner and others climbed into parked vehicles. There was a small taxi stand a few blocks down the street but Smith couldn't see it from his vantage point.

It was Jorge's cab that he was interested in and it hadn't moved since he and his lady friend went into the club. The thumping faded and more people exited the club. The target and his woman left by themselves. Aided by Jorje, the woman wobbled badly as she walked. It might have had something to do with high heels on cobblestone because she stopped and kicked them off.

She almost fell on her face while stooping to pick them up and Jorje yanked back on her arm to stop her from going down. Not impressed with his rough attempt to keep her upright, the woman broke away from him and turned to walk in the opposite direction. He caught up to her just as she was about to take a nosedive into the pavement. She shouted something in Spanish and he looked around to see if anyone was watching.

The woman's legs appeared to have become rubber and Jorge took most of her weight with his shoulder, his arm wrapped around her waist. He almost had to drag her to his car, where he poured her into the back seat. Smith tensed. He felt an increase in his heart rate. The street light above the taxi was burnt out so he reached into his go bag for his night-vision binoculars.

Jorge started his car and drove away before he could get them out. He headed directly out of town and turned right onto the highway, toward Cihuatlan. Smith hung way back, directed by the tracker's display on his phone. He played a variety of scenarios in his head. Was Jorge about to claim another victim? Was he a rapist or murderer? What the American saw in those graves said he was probably both.

There was no other traffic on the road and Jorge had the pedal to the metal. He was on a mission. A flash of anger came over Smith. Where was Alvarez or his surveillance crew? Did he even arrange it? It was doubtful since they were the only two cars on the road. Even if the cops had their own tracking device, he would have spotted them at some point throughout the day.

No Ed, no backup, and no fucking cops to serve and protect. Smith was flying solo. But he was a professional and had been in worse situations. He instinctively reached to his right hip where a holster would normally sit, but he wasn't in the USA and didn't have access to a gun. Weapons came in all forms though and he had a selection of goodies stashed in his go bag.

Jorge hung a hard right off the highway, somewhere in the middle of the coconut and banana farms. Smith watched for the rusty old truck as he approached the area but it was so dark he couldn't see anything off the road. Making the turn indicated on his phone, he killed his headlights as not to be detected. He stopped for a moment to let his eyes adjust to the dark.

The taxi's taillights were barely visible in the distance and Smith continued to follow for what seemed like forever. There were no landmarks visible and he had no idea where he was. He scrolled through the contacts on his phone to find the police chief's number and hit redial but it went directly to voicemail. A wasted call but one he thought necessary if a vicious crime was about to go down.

It was Mexico and Smith was a foreigner, and accordingly he had no more rights than the piece of shit he was tailing. His heart raced faster, as if he was in a high-speed pursuit, but he stayed composed and kept his distance. Finally, the cab's brake lights came on. Smith reacted and moved his foot to his brake pedal, but thought it wiser to shift to neutral and coast to a stop.

He pulled out the night vision binoculars but was too far away to see what was happening in the taxi cab. The PI shifted from drive to neutral a few more times to crawl closer but then got worried Jorge might hear his engine noise. He'd have to go on foot to get near enough and hopefully catch his man in the act.

What did that mean, exactly? Did he have to let Jorge actually assault the woman to nab him while committing a crime? That seemed pretty stupid but Mexico had laws too, and if there was ever going to be a court case Smith would have to act accordingly. Maybe it would be easier to drag him out of his cab and beat him to death. It seemed the perfect place to get justice.

Smith made his way to the taxi on foot by taking cover in the banana trees along the left side of the dirt road. Every so many yards, he popped his head out and peered through the binoculars. He was still over a hundred yards away when he noticed Jorge was in the back seat and he couldn't see the woman.

He had to act fast and time it perfectly.

CHAPTER SIXTY-SIX

In Progress

When John Smith got close enough to see what was happening in the back seat of the taxicab he didn't have time to think about a plan of action. Seeing Jorge on top of the woman tearing at her clothes, instinct took over. He'd been brought up to respect and protect women. What was taking place in the car enraged him.

The American charged the driver's side of the car and pulled on the rear door handle but it was locked. His feet against that door, Jorge heard the latch and turned to look over his shoulder. Without a second thought, Smith threw an elbow into the window in an attempt to break it but only bounced off. The Mexican was still on top of the woman but reached under the front seat, fumbling to find something.

Smith wound up and elbowed the window again, this time shattering the glass. Jorge was still reaching under the driver's seat when he was grabbed by the legs. The PI didn't even bother to open the door and he dragged the rapist feet-first through the window. Jorge clawed at his victim and the car's interior, trying to take hold of anything that would keep him inside the car.

As if pulling a newborn calf from its mother's womb, Smith yanked him out from the back seat of the taxi. Jorge's head appeared last and followed his body to the ground. He'd barely touched down, when the angry American picked him up with both hands wrapped around his neck. Unable to breathe and dangling with his feet off the ground, Jorge saw his attacker for the first time, face to face.

He had no idea who the gringo was. His lungs screaming for air, Jorge swung his fists wildly at the man's head. Landing only glancing blows, he used his feet and managed to find the stranger's groin. He appeared to be American, with lighter skin than his own. His arms were muscular and strong but his testicles were as sensitive as every other man's.

A loosened grip on his throat allowed Jorje to suck in some air, and with it a slight burst of energy. The man groaned, giving away his pain, the Mexican's chance to fight back. He reached over the stranger's arms and stuck both thumbs in his eye sockets. That forced the gringo's head back but it didn't loosen the grip on his neck, his airway was still cut off.

Jorge felt like a puppet, dangling in the air with someone else controlling his movement. Unsure why, he remembered a move his favorite Luchador made to get out of a similar situation. He pulled his arms back and then threw his hands forward, boxing the gringo's ears. That stunned the man and caused him to release the hold on his throat. Jorge fell to the ground and his attacker took a few steps back.

Surprised, but not defeated, Smith caught the Mexican in a headlock when he lunged forward attempting to tackle him. Using the momentum, he spun Jorge around and slammed his head into the driver's door of the taxi. He repeated the move several more times until the rapist went limp in his arms and flumped to the ground like a bag of wet cement.

Still wound and enraged, Smith kicked Jorge a few times for good measure, making sure he was down for the count. A bit off-balance, he massaged his ringing ears and reached down to make sure everything was still in the right place. He knew from previous encounters that his aching balls would take some time to recover.

The woman in the back seat of the taxi never moved the whole time he was fighting with Jorge. Smith leaned inside the car, shook and tried to arouse her. It appeared she was unconscious, possibly drugged, there was no way to be sure. Her clothes were torn and disheveled but it seemed the rapist failed to complete his mission. The American was thankful for that but wasn't sure what to do next.

He called Chief Alvarez.

CHAPTER SIXTY-SEVEN

Cleanup

Jorge the rapist was conscious but lying prone on the ground with his hands and feet zip-tied when the police arrived. A truckload of heavily-armed Federals escorted the police chief to the scene of the crime. The soldiers surrounded John Smith and Jorge at gunpoint until Alvarez casually strolled up to the two combatants.

He took in both men, then turned to the open rear passenger door of the taxi cab. A barely conscious woman sat there staring into the empty space in front of her. Upon seeing the police chief, Jorge immediately went into a tirade in Spanish. Alvarez pretended to listen for a moment, then kicked him in the middle of his back.

The chief said something to the soldiers pointing their guns at Smith and they joined their comrades in focusing their attention on Jorge. The American took it as his cue to fill in the chief about the assault he witnessed on the woman in the back of the taxi. Alvarez listened intently, breaking eye contact intermittently, while he considered his options.

Smith saw the reaction and thought it was a no-brainer. Arrest the bad guy for attempted rape and take him to jail. But the chief seemed to have something else on his mind. He motioned for the PI to join him at the front of the taxi, away from the others. "Have you spoken to the woman...is she willing to make a formal complaint?"

"Did you look at her? She's still out of it...roofied, I'd say."

The chief nodded. "You mean the date-rape drug?"

"That, or something else to render her unconscious...I didn't see her put up any kind of a fight and she was out cold when I pulled Jorge off of her."

Alvarez scratched his chin, still in thought. "Yes, I see...you did some damage to the window and door...and Jorge too. You will have to account for those injuries and someone will have to be responsible for the..."

Smith cut him off. "Are you kidding me? I stopped that asshole from raping a woman and he resisted arrest...it was self-defense on my part. Pissed off, he kicked sand towards the taxi.

"I'm just saying, senor, that Jorge has friends who may want retribution or restitution...if you know what I mean. Some type of payment may be necessary to smooth things over with those friends."

John Smith knew exactly what the chief was talking about, that certain people Jorge was connected to would expect justification for the action taken against him. Especially because it was not sanctioned. It really didn't matter what kind of asshole Jorge was, permission would be needed if any harm to him was intended.

The American had expected what the chief was alluding to ever since the reward was mentioned and he paid him some of the cash up front. He asked Alvarez if another fifty thousand dollars might make certain people see things for what they were, that Jorge was bad for their business and a constant thorn in their side.

The chief held back his answer until Smith retrieved a bundle of cash from his go bag and handed it over. Alvarez smiled and said the gesture should receive the appropriate response if he handled the matter himself. Obviously, the chief would be lining his own pockets before any of the cash reached the appropriate people. He yelled out a command to his soldiers. They scooped up Jorje like a sack of smashed potatoes and threw him in the back of their pickup truck.

Alvarez called the taxi company to come retrieve their vehicle and he put the woman in his car. Smith asked why he wasn't having any type of forensic examination done on the cab but the chief said it wouldn't be necessary. He got in his police car and drove off with the victim. As Smith climbed into his rental, he could still hear Jorge shouting obscenities from down the road.

CHAPTER SIXTY-EIGHT

Season's End

The arrest of the notorious Jorge pretty well brought a conclusion to our murder club. That and it was the end of the tourist season, with many of us snowbirds having left or getting ready to migrate back to our northern homes. It had been a productive three months for me as a writer, having completed about two thirds of my next novel.

Our little club was a fun distraction, for the most part. Some enjoyed it more than others. John Smith didn't wait around for any fallout that might come his way from Jorge's cartel connections. He had another job waiting for him back home but spent his last night in Melaque getting drunk with his new circle of friends. The women were especially sad to see him go.

With the club's disbanding, many questions remained unanswered. There were still people missing with no explanations as to their whereabouts. We heard nothing further from police or any other authorities regarding the human remains found in the lagoon. Rumor was some had been identified and others never would. The sad truth is it was Mexico and we expected that.

For those of us still in town, we decided to have a farewell party at Twiggs bar. There was to be a fantastic show of meteors and meteorites zooming by and entering earth's atmosphere. Not that we needed an excuse for a party, but most folks still at the resort said they were interested. The only challenge for us seniors was to stay up past dark but luckily it came fairly early at that time of year.

Knowing there was no food service at Twiggs, a few of the gang threw together a hasty barbeque to get something in our stomachs to absorb the booze we'd no doubt be consuming. Since the bar was at the far end of town, we piled into three vehicles to make the trip. The sun was just setting when we arrived. We'd seen the brilliant end of day colors many times but it was like watching your favorite movie over and over.

There was time to kill before the anticipated meteor show so we either hung out at the driftwood bar or sat around one of the fire pits. I found a discarded wood picture frame and we took turns photographing each other for fun.

Bruce patiently watched a bartender rolling a joint and asked if he could buy one. The man offered it for free and only asked to be considered when tipping for drinks.

Big Willy and Wanda hammed it up, posing inside the driftwood heart on the beach, expertly positioned to take in the sunset.

Fred and Wilma talked to a young couple with an expensive-looking dune buggy.

GP and Helen sat quietly on a bench, enjoying the ocean breeze and sound of waves rolling ashore.

Sticks sat on a bar swing, letting her toes drag in the sand as she swayed back and forth.

Tommy and Morty engaged in a private conversation at the far end of the bar. Their women nearby somewhere.

Katie and I joined in the picture taking on the beach and I listened for the hissing sound when the sun kissed the water. It slipped below the surface as quickly as our three winter months had passed by. As much as I hated the sand, watching the sunset at the beach was hard to beat.

When Helen called out that she saw a shooting star, we scrambled to grab a drink and find a good seat to view the upcoming event. Chairs and benches consisted of driftwood or cut tree trunks and logs and weren't very comfortable. Considering my aching back, I cursed under my breath and wondered why we didn't bring our own chairs. If I had a blanket, and knew I would be able to get up again, I would have laid on the sand.

Willy brought up how close the bathrooms were to the lagoon and wondered if the crocodiles ever wandered into them. GP told him not to scare the women and the johns were built on stilts that the critters couldn't climb. Tommy laughed and asked if anyone had ever seen how fast they can run. Katie grabbed my arm and said she'd rather pee in the bushes.

The conversation digressed to other scary stories that were more fiction than fact. Morty said he once responded to a call for a big snake that came up from someone's toilet and bit a woman's ass. Fred turned to Wilma and asked if Morty was talking about anal intercourse. Sticks spewed her drink and almost fell off her log.

A shooting star or passing meteor caught Katie's attention and she called it out. Everyone stared into the star-studded sky waiting for a repeat. Bruce pointed out the dippers, Orion's belt and what he thought were Venus and Mars. Then, out of nowhere, a huge black cloud appeared over Isla de Navidad blocking our view of the sky behind the mountain.

Tommy pointed it out, saying he hadn't been back there golfing since Gary disappeared on the twelfth hole. He added that Gary planned to return to the links but hadn't quite gotten there yet.

Willy asked, "Who can blame him?"

I mentioned strange black clouds had been reported along with UFO sightings in the past.

Katie elbowed me. "Now you're trying to scare us, Ed."

GP scoffed. "Next you're going to tell us the meteorites are actually spaceships coming to earth?"

I tilted my head. "Just saying...more and more of that stuff is being uncovered and released to the media every day. You worked for the government, GP, you believe everything they say?"

"Point taken."

Helen asked, "You really believe, Ed?"

I kept my gaze on the sky. "I believe we're not the only life forms in this vast universe we're part of...there's too many planets and solar systems and stars and galaxies that we can't even see and have no idea about. They're finding things now on our own planet that point to ancient civilizations thousands of years before any of our ancestors were around. Experts can't explain who or what they were."

Bruce cut in. "Ed's right. I've read about that...ancient technology that can't be explained...like the true function of the pyramids. Scientists would have you believe they were built as tombs but have never discovered any bodies in them. And now there's proof they might have been some kind of electrical plants...something Tesla was onto."

GP scoffed again but he was interrupted by a bright flash in the sky, an actual fireball screaming towards earth.

CHAPTER SIXTY-NINE

Grand Finale

I'd seen shooting stars before and even a meteor similar to this one. But instead of zooming across the sky to a destination somewhere else on earth, this one appeared to be heading in our direction. Everyone on the beach fell silent as the extraterrestrial object grew closer. The little hairs on my neck and arms stood up. Were we about to witness a splashdown somewhere nearby in the ocean?

I expected sound from something travelling at that speed and coming so close to us but there was only silence. No one spoke, the ocean grew still. The meteorite momentarily disappeared behind the ominous black cloud that still shrouded Isla de Navidad. There was a flash—a brilliant strobe of light that caused everyone to shield their eyes.

The music stopped. Every light in the area went dark. The moonless sky came alive with the brightest star display I'd ever seen. Some of the gang whispered to each other. Katie gripped my arm so tight, her nails dug into my skin. The lights flickered and came back on but dead silence still hung in the air.

I heard myself saying, 'Wow'. Others chimed in.

Tommy thought the fireball hit the back of the island, maybe the golf course or marina.

Willy thought it landed further out in the ocean.

Sticks said there was an oil platform out that way and maybe the bright light was an explosion there.

GP told her the chances of that were a trillion to one.

Bruce said he needed a drink and he headed for the bar. When he turned to leave a black cat tore across the sandy patio behind us.

I heard dogs barking in the distance. Trudi and Rudi's dog, Boots, joined in. Even little Coco was disturbed and growled.

Helen said she'd never heard that before and picked the dog up.

A woman's scream drowned out the barking. She came running from the bathrooms shouting about a big crocodile chasing her. The elderly female moved almost as fast as the black cat. She ran right out of the bar and down the road to town. She wasn't crazy, a crocodile about the size of my Harley Davidson headed towards the bar.

There was shouting and screaming as everyone cleared the bar and tried to figure which way was best to go. Our gang stayed near the fire pit on the beach, hoping that would keep the big boy at bay. It appeared he might belly up to the bar but the crocodile crawled on past and headed for the ocean. Nervous laughter broke out all around.

Tommy said he'd never seen anything like the meteorite or crazy crocodile and he was buying a round of tequila shots. He returned with a tray of little glasses and we all said, 'Salud' to a great and eventful night.

The music came back on and Katie said she wanted to dance.

Trudi walked up to our circle and asked if we'd seen Rudi.

Sticks said she saw him at the bar with Bruce, before the crocodile incident. Just then, her little dog ran up to Trudi with its leash in tow and no Rudi. We all could see that he and Bruce weren't at the bar so their women went to look for them. They came back and said the bartender saw the two men wander off in the direction of the bright light.

CHAPTER SEVENTY

Homeward Bound

Most of our group were to leave town over the next week or so. Bruce and Rudi were still missing. Morty reached out to Chief Alvarez about their disappearance. He said they weren't the only two reported missing after the meteorite sighting and he'd also received dozens of calls for strange animal incidents. We were all perplexed by our two friends' disappearance. Sticks was beside herself and unsure if she should head back home alone.

Morty called again while we were heading out. He had more news from Alvarez, who just announced his retirement and invited him out on his new fishing boat. He said the chief had good and bad news about Jorge. I always liked to hear the bad stuff first so I told him to go ahead.

Alvarez said he regretted to report that all charges against Jorge were stayed and he would not have his day in court. Even though I half expected something like that, I dropped an f-bomb and a few other expletives before asking for the good news.

Morty said that Jorge committed suicide while in jail. That made me feel a bit better. "Hung himself?" I asked.

"No, he stabbed himself fifteen times with three different shanks." Morty laughed and I happily joined in. Cop humor.

"So, justice prevailed. I'm gonna miss our breakfasts, Amigo."

"Me took, Detective. See you next season."

On the drive out of town Katie turned to me. "So, if Jorge killed those women and buried them on the farm, who do you think is responsible for all those bodies in the lagoon?"

I turned onto the highway, heading north. "I really don't know...could be anyone."

She thought about it for a minute. "I'm glad he's dead. You were a police officer for a long time...what do you think happened to Bruce and Rudi?"

I checked for traffic before merging left. I stifled a smile and half-cocked my head to the right. "You don't want to know, baby."

The End

Other Books by Edmond Gagnon

A Casual Traveler
Four - A Paranormal Thriller

Norm Strom Crime Series

Rat
Bloody Friday
Torch
Finding Hope
Border City Chronicles
Trafficking Chen
Border City Chronicles - Four More

Abigail Brown Crime Series

Moon Mask
The Millionaire Murders

Edmond Gagnon grew up in Windsor, Ontario, Canada. He joined the Windsor Police Department in 1977, a month before his nineteenth birthday. After almost two years as a police cadet, Ed was promoted to Constable and walked a beat in downtown Windsor. He spent the next thirteen years in uniform, working the street.

From there, he transferred to plain clothes where he worked in narcotics, vice, property crimes, fraud, and arson. He was promoted to Sergeant, then Detective. During that time, Ed investigated everything from theft and burglary to arson and murder. He retired with a total of thirty-one years and four months of service.

Within weeks of retirement, Ed took to travelling the world, visiting countries in Southeast Asia and South America as well as riding his motorcycle all over Canada and the United States. He kept in touch with family and friends through email, sending them snippets and stories of his adventures.

The recipients of his musings suggested he write a book about his travels and Ed put together a collection of short stories in his first book, *A Casual Traveler*.

Bitten by the writing bug, Ed decided to share some of his police stories. He created the Norm Strom Crime Series, inspired by events and people he encountered during his years in law enforcement. He also wrote the spinoff Abigail Brown Crime Series.

Edmond Gagnon continues to write, adding the science fiction thriller, *Four*, to his collection of novels. Ed still travels frequently and resides in Windsor, with his wife, Cathryn.

You can see all of Edmond Gagnon's books and more at: **www.edmondgagnon.com**